D1282142

THE FARM
MAX ANNAS

CATALYST PRESS
Pacifica, California

For further information,
write Catalyst Press,
or email info@catalystpress.org

In North America, this book is distributed by
Consortium Book Sales & Distribution, a division of Ingram.
Phone: 612/746-2600
cbsdinfo@ingramcontent.com
www.cbsd.com

In South Africa, Namibia, and Botswana,
this book is distributed by LAPA Publishers.
Phone: 012/401-0700
lapa@lapa.co.za
www.lapa.co.za

FIRST EDITION
10 9 8 7 6 5 4 3 2 1
Library of Congress Control Number: 2020933695
ISBN: 978-1-946395-22-1

Cover design by Karen Vermeulen, Cape Town, South Africa

AUGUST 24, 5:32 PM

"I'm not racist," Franz Muller declared, pausing to study the hole in his fence.

He was wondering who had come out here with a bolt cutter during the night and done this. He was also wondering who owned the white panel van that was parked beside the front door. Kobus Prins, the fat man standing next to him, nodded dutifully without saying a word.

"But...," Muller resumed before trailing off again. As he took a loud breath through his mouth, the first shot landed, thwack, ripping off his right earlobe.

Muller grabbed his head, feeling warm blood seep between his fingers. Thwack. Prins uttered a dull Ah before sinking to his knees, his hands fumbling helplessly for the wound in his back.

Muller dropped to the ground and watched as Prins was hit one more time. Muller yanked the sales rep down to the ground. Prins coughed up blood all over the farmer before crumpling on top of him. The two dogs leaped over both men.

Prins was dead, lying on his stomach on top of Muller. The farmer wrenched his head around and caught sight of Trixie's Hyundai next to the front door, the old Bedford bakkie sitting a little farther away. That's where the dogs had gone, terrified and cowering against each other. Thwack.

Thwack. Thwack. The white van, Jayne's little Mercedes, the large rolls of barbed wire. *Other people saw their lives flash before them*, Muller thought, *in that last moment*. He saw his property. Simonshoek was his life. Thwack. Now he was lying on his side, Prins bleeding all over him.

Trixie! Muller wondered where she was right now, as the heavy seed agent squashed the air out of him.

"Everyone inside!" he called with his last gasp of air. "Right now!"

He felt Prins' pulse, just to be sure.

Trixie! He thought again. Thwack. He had just seen his daughter somewhere on the porch. As he shifted his position a little to ease his breathing, he heard a bullet strike metal. Some car or other. He saw Thabo jump behind the rolls of barbed wire that had just been delivered this morning. Thabo dragged his stiff leg behind him a little and tried to roll up into a tight ball. Thwack.

Thwack.

Thwack.

Thwack.

A windowpane shattering. The house.

Frenzied running, bodies hitting the ground everywhere. Muller heard screams and cries.

"In here!" Trixie called.

He didn't think it was a good idea to push Prins' heavy body off his own quite yet. If there was anything protecting him in this open area between the fence and the farmhouse, it was this mass of flesh.

All of a sudden, the shots stopped. Gcilitshana

was lying on his stomach behind his car, holding a pistol. His head up. The sinking sun glimmered through the windows on the one side of the police BMW and back out the other side. The dogs were stretched out close to him, no longer moving. And then Muller caught sight of Trixie's white skirt. Underneath the Bedford, along with her feet and another pair next to those. Old shoes and dark pants. Those must belong to the boy who had come to repair the fence. Thwack. A pane in the bakkie exploded. The feet behind it began dodging away from the car skeleton. *Stay put*, Muller thought. *You won't find a better shield.*

More feet joined those. He had forgotten about the three workers. The first of them dashed out from behind the Bedford. A target in overalls, perfectly illuminated by the last sunbeam. Thwack. He reached the house with a final jump. The second took off after him, followed by the third. Thwack. Thwack. Thwack. Thwack. The bullets buried themselves in the van. The two men also reached the house in safety.

One more minute and it would be much darker. Hopefully, no one would do anything stupid. Gcilitshana slowly got to his knees and peered through his car window in the direction the shots were coming. Had to be about twenty so far. Or less.

Or more. Who was behind this? It only took a couple thousand rands to arrange for a quick hit or two. And they would also find the folks in the house. But why had they come today of all days? When so many people were around?

Gcilitshana stretched his arm across the BMW's hood, his fingers curled around his service pistol. The daylight was almost gone. The policeman glanced over at Muller and gave a quick nod. He began to shoot at one-second intervals. Eight times. He stood up and dashed for the front door. No return fire. Muller rolled Prins' body to the side but stayed where he was. Luckily, Zak had turned off the motion detector. His son was reliable.

Muller could just make out the feet underneath the Bedford. Something was moving over there. Now the repair guy emerged from behind the vehicle. He ran holding Trixie by the hand. No shots. As they reached the door, Trixie stumbled, but the boy deftly yanked her inside.

Muller was the only one left outdoors. It was practically dark, and inside the house, they would be getting nervous. He imagined holding his Walther. He would go back outside and take care of each one of them. He crawled slowly toward the front door, but suddenly he'd had enough of all this crap. After all, it was as good as dark. He stood up and covered the final meters upright. As the door shut behind him, a bullet burrowed into the soft wood of the door frame, right next to him. He hadn't even heard the gun fire.

The farmer gripped the inside doorknob with both hands and felt astonished. He hadn't even thought of his wife once since the first shot had hit.

AUGUST 24, 5:58 PM

Thabo Buti prevented Rosie Muller from going to the door to look out. The people who had just made it inside and those who had been watching the shootout from indoors were gathered behind them. The boss was the last one in the house, and he was now leaning against the door, his shirt drenched in blood. Thabo pulled him away from the entrance.

"We have no idea how many bullets they have! They won't hold anything back." He rapped his knuckle against the wood, then pushed the first of the locks in place.

"There's no point to doing that! They'll get inside if they want to!" Mrs. Muller pushed Trixie and Thabo aside to reach her husband. "Thank heaven nothing happened," she said as she tried to hug Franz Muller, who brushed aside the attempted embrace.

The second lock bolt was sticking. Thabo had to use his fist to get the hinge to latch. The other two bolts were mounted so far down that he had to stretch his stiff leg out to the side to bend down far enough. When he was done, he pulled himself up by the doorknob, before gazing into the spacious foyer now suffused with twilight. The entire group was standing there, their eyes fixed on him and the Mullers.

"Of course, something happened," the farmer retorted. "They got Prins!"

This was no surprise to those who'd been outside. Mrs. Muller inhaled sharply.

"The pigs!" Zak replied.

The younger of Trixie's girls started to cry. Was her name Christina? The older one tried to comfort her. Britney? Thabo couldn't tell the two of them apart anymore, not since Muller's daughter had cut their hair.

"Zak, turn off the kitchen light." Muller opened the curtains over the little window next to the door and looked out. "How's the phone?"

"Dead," Zak said.

Muller nodded. "And the cell service?"

Thabo checked his screen. No bars. He watched as the dirty cop, Trixie and Zak studied their phones as well. Sometimes you could get reception out here, but not usually. Standing behind them were Cesar, Sipho and Jo-Jo, who'd been up to God knew what, as well as simple Betsie in her smock, which she called "my uniform." The young repair guy, who was here because of the fence, stood next to her. Thabo had never set eyes on the man beside them, the one in the black jeans and black shirt with a name tag on his chest. Mrs. McKenzie, Mrs. Muller's friend, was way at the back, leaning against the wall.

"Check the house," Muller ordered Thabo. "See if anyone is hiding. Look in every room! But no lights. Is the gate shut?"

Thabo nodded. The gate had closed automatically, right after the first shots had been fired. He walked up to the second floor. Zak's room was adjacent to the staircase. The unmade bed, the clothes strewn everywhere. Nobody would hide in there. Who would come up here anyway? The danger was clearly coming from the outside. Whoever was out there behind a bush or a tree and taking potshots at them had nothing to do with the people inside the house.

He opened the door to Trixie's room. No need to knock. Everyone was down in the entry hall. Spic and span. Thabo picked up a lacy red slip from a pile of freshly ironed laundry and sniffed it. Soapy fresh. He had to chuckle. Twenty years ago, he would have been whipped for that. By Muller himself. Childish chaos reigned in the small guest room. The large guest room was locked, and both bathrooms were empty. He very cautiously opened the door to the Mullers' bedroom. He had never been in here, over all the years. Betsie took care of the work in there. Every pillow and doily in its place. Thabo knew that Muller's safe was hidden somewhere in this room. The mid-sized guest room looked like an ad for a hotel in East London he'd once seen. There was only one room left. Mrs. Muller's prayer room. Thabo believed in God, and in Jesus Christ as well. He also believed that God had intended for people to have better lives. However, what Mrs. Muller did in here day after day, that really was too much. A life-sized Jesus hung from a cross on the wall, a kneeler sitting below it. And a whole lot of pictures on the walls of people he didn't know and who looked like they'd been dead for a long time. Probably saints. No Africans among them. Not even one.

Back downstairs, Zak and Gcilitshana were shoving a large wardrobe in front of the living room window. Thabo's eyes had grown accustomed to the dark.

"Sit down over there, both of you!" Trixie ordered, pointing her girls into the farthest corner of the living room.

Mrs. Muller and Mrs. McKenzie were sitting on the large couch. The three workers stood around like they were waiting to be picked up any minute. Trixie knelt down beside her children. The repair guy and the man in black chatted in the doorway between the foyer and the living room.

"Okay. Everyone in here!" Muller was the boss, and he was standing behind his wife with his hands on the back of the sofa. Everyone moved reluctantly into the middle of the giant room.

Zak pushed the wardrobe one last centimeter against the window, which was now almost completely covered. There were other smaller windows and another large one in the door to the terrace, but the wardrobe would protect them from where the shots had seemingly come.

Zak rubbed his hands on his shorts and glanced around the group. "I knew we'd eventually get hit. We're so far out here. And now it's our turn. It's always just a matter of time. No one protects the farmers. All we do is make sure people have something to eat."

"Calm down, Mr. Muller." Gcilitshana. "Don't forget I'm here."

"You ran like everyone else." Trixie. "And Zak's right. Thousands of farmers have already been murdered."

"God be with us." Mrs. Muller.

"Could all of you just shut up?" Muller. "Alfred. Do you know what's going on?"

Thabo sank into an unoccupied armchair. Gcilitshana searched for words. The smaller girl began to cry again. The policeman took a deep breath: "Well, we don't know what's happening here..."

Trixie jumped up. "You've got a radio. Where is it?"

Gcilitshana looked at her, annoyed. "In my car. And if our cell phones aren't working, it won't either. So...have there been any conflicts here lately? Any arguments?"

"You're crazy!" Zak jumped at the policeman. "That has nothing to do with this."

"Zak!" Muller's strident voice silenced the boy. "Keep going, Alfred!"

Cesar, one of the three workers, watched Thabo, his eyes anxious. Thabo raised his hand to keep him quiet. Soon.

Gcilitshana hemmed and hawed a bit before continuing. "Look, we won't really know what's going on till we catch these guys. Maybe they've already hightailed it to some tavern in Mdantsane and are getting plastered. How long has it been since the last shot was fired?"

"Exactly!" Mrs. Muller. "They're long gone."

Her last syllable was cut off by exploding glass. A bullet soared through the small space between the wardrobe and the window frame, shredding the armrest of the chair in which Thabo was sitting and burrowing into the wood. He felt the chair tremble. Everyone either jumped up or leaped aside. Trixie threw herself across her children with a shriek. Thabo didn't even get up. What else could he do?

"We have to arm ourselves," a woman's voice

broke in.

It took Thabo a few seconds to realize that this sentence had been uttered by Mrs. McKenzie, Mrs. Muller's pious friend.

AUGUST 24, 6:33 PM

"Franz," Mrs. Muller said, breathlessly. "Did you hear what Jayne just suggested?"

"I'm not deaf!"

"And?"

"I'll only give guns to people I trust."

Thabo knew what that meant. Only to white people. And maybe him. And the dirty cop.

Gcilitshana grunted.

"Exactly!" Zak replied.

"Besides, I don't have all that many."

That was nonsense. Muller owned an arsenal, large enough to attack and conquer Mozambique.

A burst of gunfire splintered the window behind the wardrobe. The bullets thudded dully into the wood. Trixie screamed.

"Shit! Is anyone hit?" Muller bellowed. When nobody answered, he hollered again. "You, over there! Who are you? What do you want here?"

"I'm from Quick Trans. I'm just here to deliver a package." That had to be the guy in black.

"It's okay, Dad." Zak. "For me. It was for me. My hard drives."

Another window shattered. Very close by. Thabo jumped up. The shots were now coming from two sides.

Screams. More shots. Shards of glass. Thabo trampled somebody's feet before he found a spot against the wall next to the window through which the bullets had just been fired. Someone groaned.

"I'm hurt!" a voice exclaimed. It was the one that had just been speaking. The delivery boy.

"They're coming!" The cop. "We have to defend ourselves! We need the guns, Muller!"

"Franz! The guns!" Mrs. McKenzie. "We have to fight back!"

"Yes, Franz!" Mrs. Muller.

Both girls were sobbing now.

"Miss Trixie," Thabo interjected. "You need to take the children upstairs. They'll be safer there!"

"Come on, Muller, hurry up!" Gcilitshana urged. "Where are you, Muller?"

Footsteps on glass. "I'll be right back." Zak. "Come with me."

AUGUST 24, 6:41 PM

Gclitshana watched over Thabo's shoulder as he tried to calm Trixie. The farm foreman stood in the door frame as he spoke to the young woman.

"Go lie down with the children, Miss Trixie. Help them feel better. We'll take care of everything else." He shut the door.

"Is the cell service always so bad out here?"

Thabo nodded. "Usually."

Two shots. No hits. They gazed at each other for a moment and sat down at the top of the staircase. Gcilitshana studied Thabo. He was relatively well-dressed, had shown himself adept with the young woman, and only spoke when he actually had something to say. His shirt had seen better days, but every morning, he pulled it out of his closet, clean and ironed. The cop suspected this was the product of a long marriage and several decades spent on Muller's farm.

"Has there been any trouble around here before now?" Gcilitshana knew his question sounded stupid, but he wanted to get Thabo talking.

"Never!"

"Not even a break-in?"

"Not since I've been here."

Gcilitshana waited.

"That's been over thirty years."

"So who might be out there?"

"There haven't been many attacks in these parts."

Gcilitshana nodded, although he knew better. The police spokesperson for the Buffalo City Metropolitan Municipality had been told to work the actual figures into the current statistics. Burglary. Property damage. Assault. Armed robbery. Murder. Only when it was absolutely impossible for him to conceal the information did he inform the press that a farm had been attacked. When a murder occurred, there wasn't much that could be covered up, of course. "But who could it be?" he asked.

"I wonder why they're taking such long breaks. They could've just shot everything up."

"Maybe not. They might not be the best shooters."

"But why are they taking such a long break again?"

"Something's come up."

"What?"

"Too many people at the farm. How much money is usually lying around here?"

"A lot. Several thousand, all the time."

"Nobody'd pay for an attack for so little cash."

"How many are out there?"

"I don't know. Perhaps more than we think."

"What do they want?"

"No clue. More than a few thousand rands. Who was the fat white guy who got shot out there?"

"Prins. Sales rep. Sold seeds. Stopped by twice a year. The boss always served him good wine and cigars."

"Why does anyone have to buy seeds?"

"Don't ask me. It's been like that here for a long time. The boss swears by it."

"Who else is here? Besides the family."

"The delivery boy. The one who got hurt."

Shots. Shattering glass. No screams.

"Who else?"

"You!"

"Hmm. Besides me."

"The guy here to fix the fence."

"What's wrong with the fence?"

"There was a hole in it this morning. And also three of my workers. And Mrs. McKenzie."

"What does she do?"

"She prays with Mrs. Muller."

"She makes special trips out here for that?"

"From Gonubie."

"That's sixty kilometers!"

"Trixie and the children aren't here all the time, either."

"Uh-huh. Something's not right. Why didn't they wait until the delivery boy and the sales rep left? And the repair guy?"

"Prins wouldn't have left for a while."

"The wine?"

"And the cigars."

"Who did they actually see outside?"

Thabo thought for a moment. "The two of us. Boss Muller. Miss Trixie. The workers. The young repair guy. And Prins, the sales rep."

"Uh-huh. So they didn't see Zak. And the delivery boy. And Mrs. Muller. And that, uh, McKenzie."

"And Betsie. And the children. And..."

"Yes?"

"Vuyo was also here. Betsie's son. But I haven't seen him for a few hours."

They could hear Muller and his son at the bottom of the stairs. Despite the darkness, Gcilitshana thought he could see that their arms were full of guns.

"Where are the guns kept?" Gcilitshana asked.

"In a hole in the office floor."

"Locked?"

"Locked."

"A lot of them?"

"Tons."

Gcilitshana thought about old Roelf Botha, only a year or so from retirement. So sick that he didn't necessarily have to work. But he wanted to. Which was why Botha kept in touch with the conservative white farmers. Like Muller. But today he had to be at the oncology office again. *That's the only reason I'm here*, Gcilitshana thought. *Because of his cancer. Otherwise I'd be putting my feet up at KFC.*

"Okay," he said, getting to his feet. "The young woman and the children are upstairs. Who else in the house can help us?"

Thabo also stood up. "Muller and Zak. My workers. You. And me. All the men actually. The delivery boy's the only one hurt."

"Hmm. We should go downstairs. We need to talk about how we're going to survive this."

AUGUST 24, 6:41 PM

From here, the view was still good, even though it had grown quite dark. But at the spot where the sun had just dropped, there was a thin, lingering bar of light. And the moon was already high in the sky.

Nobody had said there'd be so many people. Once he'd shot the fat man, everything was supposed to go really quickly. Should have gone really quickly. They would have returned fire, but he would have finished them off. And then everything would have been over in just a few minutes.

Instead, they were all holed up in the house. That wouldn't help anyone, though. They'd eventually be dead. All of them.

However, he was already worrying a little about his people's lives. To be more precise: his own life. The contract had been to come here, shoot, grab the stuff, and get back out again.

There'd probably be victims on both sides now. He just had to make sure he wasn't one of them.

AUGUST 24, 6:41 PM

"Go lie down with the children, Miss Trixie. Help them feel better. We'll take care of everything else." Thabo shut the door.

Christina was already asleep. Britney wasn't far behind. And Trixie's eyes were filled with tears. Ever since she'd shaved her girls' heads because of the lice they'd caught at the preschool, they had looked like...how did they put it in the US? White trash? Like poor whites anyway. Like children from the trailer park. And yet she worked for a jewelry shop.

Trixie thought about her previous visit to the farm. How she had stood there at the stoplight in King William's Town, that run-down, backwater town. She hadn't been thinking anything negative when she saw that...that thief. He had grabbed a SPAR bag out of the open hatch of a station wagon and walked off. He couldn't see the officer standing on the next corner, but she did.

Then everything went terribly fast. She calls to the cop. The cop yells after the thief. The thief starts to run. A police bakkie suddenly appears. The thief tosses away the bag. The woman who owns the station wagon shows up and begins to shriek. People dash after the thief. The thief runs and can run fast. But that doesn't help him when he tries to cross the road to East London. The truck simply runs him down. And then he is dead.

The next day, her name was in the newspaper. And now they were coming to get her. All because of that one thief.

AUGUST 24, 6:45 PM

When Franz and Zak returned with the guns, Rosie Muller was leaning against the wall that separated the living room from the bathroom. You had to go through the hall to reach the bathroom, and she had picked this spot because it was far away from where the bullets were striking.

Rosie Muller didn't feel safe, but over her sixty years, she'd learned that it always paid in the end to count on God. On God and on Franz. They had already survived several incidents out here. And with Jesus Christ as her witness, that hadn't been all that easy. Like years ago, when their farm had sat on the homeland border. And the two soldiers had showed up on their doorstep. At that time, the farms hadn't been as secure as they were now. Soldiers in Ciskei uniforms. It had been the middle of the night, and they hadn't been there to ask the time. Or for directions. They were too heavily armed for that.

But they were also drunk. And too noisy. Franz had shot them. Two police officers came out the next morning from King—two white officers— and took the bodies away. They never heard anything else about the incident.

You couldn't solve problems so easily these days, not since the blacks had taken over.

AUGUST 24, 6:45 PM

Muller had a hard time getting used to the dark after he stepped into the living room. In the office, they had lowered the shades, lit their cigarette lighters, and opened the hole in the floor where the guns were concealed. Muller had selected the ones he thought most suitable before counting them out. Guns for him and Zak, as well as Thabo and Gcilitshana. He didn't trust the workers. Or the repair guy. The delivery boy was injured. He didn't trust Gcilitshana for that matter, but he couldn't afford to insult the man. He was up for promotion again soon. Thabo was okay. Muller was carrying four handguns and four different rifles.

Once his eyes adjusted to the dark, he realized that Trixie and the children were no longer in the living room. The cop and Thabo were also missing. Jayne was tending to the delivery boy, who was lying behind the couch. The three workers were standing close together in a safe corner. Then Gcilitshana and his foreman stepped into the room.

Zak distributed the guns. His son Zak. Even before the assault had started, he had been acting strangely. He kept glancing all around him.

The day had actually gotten off to a good start. A doctor—a real expert—had managed to calm his long-standing fears that Zak might be gay. Muller had told the doctor about everything, even about the animal torture he had repeatedly caught Zak doing during his teen years. But the doctor had said that gays don't torture animals. They don't have the nerves for it, he'd said.

Maybe Zak would eventually find the right woman. Muller knew it wasn't easy for young farmers to meet girls. But others had figured it out.

Considering the circumstances, the boy was doing relatively well. Shot through the shoulder, the bleeding had stopped. Jayne cleaned both wounds with gin, set the bandage, and then took a swig from the bottle.

Zak was in the process of handing out the guns.

"I'd also like something to shoot!" she said so loudly that everyone could hear it. "And besides, we should all be able to defend ourselves. Everyone needs a gun."

"The guns are only for the people I trust!" Franz.

"You don't trust me?"

"You know what I mean!"

"I've been shooting at the firing range for over forty years. I went hunting with Arnold when he was still alive. And I have a right to a gun. No, make that two. Give me two, just like the others."

Franz Muller coughed quietly and held the keys out to his son. "Zak, go!"

God is great, thought Jayne. *But there are situations in which you need to take care of yourself.*

The blacks stood off a little to the side. Zak looked over at them as he handed out the guns. Of course, they wouldn't be getting any. You couldn't even trust them to show up for work on time in the morning. He always ended up waiting on them.

He recalled the scratches on his cheeks. "I got rid of the bushes on the slope," he'd told Dad. "You wanted me to do that a long time ago."

Dad had considered this for a few moments and then nodded. He didn't need to explain the wounds on his face. Thorns, everyone knew about them. Nobody could see the scratches on his chest.

What had the girl possibly said? Not all that much had happened. She'd gotten away with a swollen eye, but he hadn't hit her hard. He just hadn't calculated on her fighting back.

The fact that her father was now in the house didn't make the matter any easier. He would have to take care of everything eventually.

AUGUST 24, 6:47 PM

Betsie was sitting next to the bathroom door. No bullets would reach back here any time soon. Maybe everything would be over soon. They must have taken off by now.

She was worried about Vuyo. Her son had been in the farmhouse this afternoon, but he had vanished at some point.

The Mullers didn't like him. Just because he had spent some time in prison. They would blame him for all this. And one person was already dead. That sales rep. What an arrogant jerk. During his last visit at the farm, she had dropped a plate of cake, and he had laughed at her.

Now he was dead.

And Vuyo was missing.

AUGUST 24, 6:47 PM

The people in the house won't see it coming, he thought.

"When?" The question came from beside him.

"Just wait," he said.

He wanted to give them a few more seconds before the storm broke. It was getting darker, but if there was one thing you could still see in the dying light, it was window panes. No night was ever completely black.

It had been stupid not to shoot more earlier. The fat man had been the best target. He should've finished off the old man, too, but he wasn't used to long-distance shooting.

He also hadn't expected so many brothers. He had dreamed about picking off several fat white folks. That would have fit with the information he'd received.

It wasn't that he had a problem killing blacks. There was just too little wealth to divide up. They couldn't all have a good car, meat for supper, and a girl for every other guy. Old Hope had once told him that they were trapped in a cut-throat capitalist competition. A cut-throat capitalist competition. He'd liked the ring of that.

And he'd already cut more than his fair share of throats. Even brothers. And a few sisters, too, along the way.

Inhaling deeply, he took aim and fired.

AUGUST 24, 6:48 PM

"You can't do anything," Jo-Jo said. "He'll fire you, and you know you won't get a job anywhere else."

Sipho just nodded.

Cesar Mhlaba also nodded. But it occurred to

him that you didn't have to put up with everything, either. Especially not when your own daughter has been raped. If he got out of this alive, he would do something. He would avenge Asanda.

Utter silence fell for the span of a second. Then a shot fired, and everyone heard it clearly. The bullet slammed into a wall somewhere. When they were all about to relax again, it started for real. The shots came from three sides, starting where the previous barrage had destroyed the window that looked out across the farmyard. Next, bullets burst through the window that was covered by the wardrobe. And then the wardrobe exploded into splinters.

As the first shots struck, the people standing around dropped to the floor. Those sitting on chairs covered their heads with their arms and slid off their seats. Cesar saved himself by diving between the sofa and the wall.

This was where Rosie Muller was also sitting. A bullet had punctured her temple.

AUGUST 24, 6:48 PM

For the second time that afternoon, Franz Muller found himself on the ground. Bullets obliterated what remained of the window frames and glass. The chandelier received its own blast. Muller heard it creak and shatter before it crashed onto the table. Someone screamed. Was that Betsie?

He was covered in glass fragments and wood, and could make out the sounds of automatic and semiautomatic weapons. A small shriek. Terror. A masculine voice. Or was it a woman's? Someone had been hit. *It wasn't Zak's voice*, Muller thought.

He crawled slowly toward the opening between the living room and the hallway. It was the same over here. The shots were coming in through the windows on both sides. They should have moved up to the second floor. They would be fairly safe up there. He thought about Trixie. Good thing she wasn't wandering around down here with the kids. They were safe, weren't they?

"Help!" someone cried from the living room.

The automatic guns fell silent, but they could still hear random shots being fired. A bullet struck something very close to him. He didn't want to risk looking up. They must have hit the old grandfather clock.

"Help!" He now recognized the voice of one of the workers. He was probably the one who had just been hit.

"Boss Muller! Boss Muller!" It was Cesar. He could place the voice now.

A few days ago, they had driven his daughter to the doctor. She had been assaulted. He sounded just as panicked now as he had that day. "Boss Muller? Where are you?"

The guns fell silent. One, two, three. Muller counted to ten. "What is it? I'm here."

"Come over here! Your wife."

"Dad!" That was Zak.

"Dad! Hurry!"

Muller stood up as a single shot was heard, but it didn't hit anything. He walked back into the living room where Zak was kneeling next to Rosie. He saw a long dark spot beside his wife, who was lying, lifeless on the floor.

"She's gone!" Zak said.

There wasn't enough light to see Zak's face, but Muller suspected his son was crying. He reached out to touch his son's head, then knelt down next to him.

Rosie was still very warm. He felt the gaping wound in her head. *Thirty-eight years*, he thought. They had shared thirty-eight years.

He wouldn't cry.

AUGUST 24, 6:55 PM

The house wasn't really shaking, but Trixie couldn't find an adequate comparison for what had just happened. She could feel the impact of each bullet. She was sensitive.

The girls were petrified with fright, but they weren't sobbing any more. They had both slept a little, waking up when the shooting began. They were clinging tightly to her—Christina to her stomach and chest, Britney around her neck. They were squeezing her so hard that Trixie could hardly breathe.

Thank God the black man who had died in King hadn't been from their farm. Or from one of the neighboring farms. But of course, they all knew each other. He had worked somewhere in the area.

Dad had said things like this happened. When she had mentioned her idea of visiting the dead man's family, he had lost his temper.

"Anyone who steals has to pay the price."

"But he has children," she had said.

"Everyone has kids," Dad had replied.

She considered this, but nothing else came to her. And then Dad had gone outside. And she hadn't been able to do anything else.

When she heard the footsteps on the stairs, she knew the end was near. One time, Gordon had forced her to watch a film in which the dead came back to life. He had laughed the whole time. What a horrible movie.

It took a few moments for Trixie to realize that the others were coming upstairs.

And either way, Gordon was an asshole. He and that bitch could just go to hell.

Someone knocked on the door.

AUGUST 24, 6:54 PM

The Boss was silent, as was everyone else. They could hear the birds and crickets outside.

The shooting had stopped. Nonetheless, Thabo Buti was still pressed against an outside wall. The walls were sufficiently strong. No bullet could get through them. He was safe here.

They had all just seen where nobody should sit. They'd gotten Mrs. Muller.

He had no idea who "they" actually were. South African farms were often attacked, but not like this. Especially not when there were so many people around. *Maybe it wasn't about the money*, Thabo thought.

But then, what was it about?

He could only think of one other motive. Revenge.

The Boss had blood on his hands, no doubt about that. He was glad he didn't know about half of what had gone down on the farm since he'd started working here. And that was practically his entire life.

Muller started to weep. The Boss. Crying. Unbelievable.

Even more incredible was Thabo's realization that he felt absolutely nothing. Neither Mrs. Muller's death nor his boss's pain mattered to him.

"We have to get out of here!"

Thabo turned around to see who was speaking. It was the dirty cop. He also was leaning against an exterior wall.

"We have to get upstairs! We aren't safe here anymore!" he continued.

"We'll be safe on the stairs." That was Mrs. McKenzie. Her voice was very low. "We can't just run through the hall as a group, though, and we won't be safe from the bullets until we reach the third or fourth step."

"Okay." Gcilitshana said. "What should we do?"

"We should crawl. All in a row. And when someone reaches the foot of the stairs, they should hurry a little."

"Alright," Gcilitshana said. "Who goes first?"

"Why not you?"

Silence descended for a few seconds. The Boss was done crying.

"Fine, I'll do it," Gcilitshana said. He dropped to the floor and crawled over to the stairs in the hall, before disappearing.

"Let's meet in the prayer room," McKenzie said. "There's only one window in there. Can the injured man make it on his own?"

"Yes," a voice replied.

AUGUST 24, 7:03 PM

Mr. Muller led his daughter from the guest room into the prayer room, the children in tow. Gcilitshana was standing with his back against the wall next to the window.

He had found the safest spot, but now felt the need to say something. He was a relatively high-ranking officer, experienced in crisis situations, and trained in every imaginable firearm. But he couldn't think of anything to say.

After the door closed, an entire minute passed before someone even cleared their throat. He thought that was Zak. He was now sidelined, as was Muller. Gcilitshana had heard more of Muller than he had seen of him since his wife's death. He couldn't be the leader himself. Only a few blacks came into question. Maybe the foreman. And of the whites...not many were left. Trixie was weak. He could see that. But what about McKenzie?

Zak cleared his throat again.

"We have to do something." That was Thabo.

"We should go out and kill them all." Zak.

Nobody replied to that. Gcilitshana chalked that up to agreement on the one hand and confusion on the other. Everyone wanted this to happen, but no one knew how to achieve that.

"Yes! Let's attack!" A woman's voice.

Gcilitshana heard gulps and groans. That must have been McKenzie's voice.

"But how?" A different woman's voice. Trixie.

"That's just crazy."

"Where is Vuyo anyway?" Muller.

"I don't know, Boss." The answer was instantaneous. Gcilitshana recalled the awkward woman in the smock. "I've been wondering that this whole time. He was still around this afternoon. He didn't tell me bye, though. He never does that. You can't think he's mixed up in this. I'm worried about him, but he wouldn't do something like this."

"Drop it," McKenzie said. "I don't know him, but he wouldn't shoot up a house with his mother in it. What was wrong with the fence, Franz?"

Muller hesitated before answering. "A hole. Cut during the night with a small-gauge cutter."

"What's missing?"

"Not much. Maybe nothing."

"The dogs?"

"Didn't hear anything."

"So they knew the intruders."

"Possibly."

"But that doesn't help us any," McKenzie said.

Gcilitshana felt like he needed to join the discussion. "So what do you think would help?"

"Attacking."

"But it's dark!" he said.

"True, but not just for us."

"How many do you think are out there?" Gcilitshana didn't recognize the voice. Perhaps one of the workers.

"Ten," he said. "Or so."

"There aren't that many of them." McKenzie. "Definitely five, maybe six. Possibly seven. But no more than that. Unless someone is just sitting out there, watching. But I don't think there are many more than six shooters out there."

"What makes you so sure?" Zak.

"We had time to listen. Two south of us. The first shots came from that way." McKenzie gestured in that direction. "When Prins was killed. I think there are two others to the west. They fired into the living room as well." She paused, then pointed in the other direction. "Fewer shots came from the north. And the shots that reached the hall didn't come through the living room." She now pointed through the window. "That makes six."

Nobody said a word.

"I might be wrong."

Murmuring, assent.

"So what should we do?" Muller.

"Let's shoot at them."

"That's insane." Zak. "We should go out guns blazing and blow them away."

"But, Zak!" Trixie.

"Be quiet." Muller. "Jayne..." Muller inhaled audibly and then exhaled. "How should we do this?"

"Very easy. There are windows all around the house, facing in every direction. We should each take up a position at one and fire whenever some-thing moves."

"But they're probably expecting that."

"Nonsense, Franz. These aren't professionals. And we have an advantage over them. We can hide better."

"But how long do you want to wait?"

"Until I see a target. When Arnold was still

alive, I used to wait with him all night long until something moved. The conditions were different, I know. We were hunting, and nobody was shooting back. But what do we have to lose?"

Gcilitshana was impressed. "Why don't you think they're professionals?"

"I'm not saying they're not tsotsis, but they can't shoot. Otherwise, we'd all be dead by now."

AUGUST 24, 7:39 PM

It was completely different than it had been with Arnold. He had simply been an enthusiastic hunter and had insisted that she accompany him. And somehow Jayne had also felt it. That rush that came when you shot another creature. Arnold had said it was a little like being God. Of course, she knew this kind of thinking was sacrilegious.

She didn't see anything at first. A totally different kind of darkness existed outside. The land rose slightly to the south. She had never noticed that the Mullers' farmhouse sat in a hollow, although she had been here so many times before.

Her eyes slowly adjusted, and she could make out some of the features in the landscape. The fence around the farmhouse was quite close. The points on the barbed wire sparkled in the weak moonlight. Jayne thought about the young repair guy. He had arrived along with her. Delivered by a white boss. How was he supposed to get home?

Franz's explanation for the hole in the fence had not been satisfactory. Had that been the first attempt by the assailants? It didn't really matter. Jayne had no idea what she had waded into out here. Either way, this wasn't a spontaneous attack, a quick in-and-out for the farmer's cash.

On the other side of the fence, Muller had
cleared an open area. "I want to see what's going
on around here," he had said once at supper. He
had arranged for everything except a grove of
apple trees to be cut down at a radius of fifty
meters from the fence line. She was slowly able
to distinguish between the bushes. They lined the
edge of the path that led to the adjacent fields.
There was a very large bush, moving gently in the
wind, with several smaller ones grouped around
it. They didn't look like they had been planted
there, more like how nature assisted by the wind
had placed them.

For the first time, Jayne looked through the
scope. The large bush leaped closer. The light
wind was causing it to sway a little. But something wasn't moving with it. Or somebody. She
was certain someone was hiding there. And she
waited.

"I'll take the side we were attacked from first,"
she had said.

Nobody had challenged her claim to the south
side. Gcilitshana, Zak and Thabo had divided up
the other three sides. Muller declined. On the
other hand, his son's gaze was bloodthirsty.

"Don't shoot until you're absolutely certain,"
Jayne had added. "Right now, we have the element of surprise on our side. Once we start shooting, we'll be in a skirmish. And we might lose."

The bathroom window on the south side was
astonishingly undamaged. Jayne cautiously turned

the latch before opening the sash quickly. It was a small window, like the kind you'd put in a townhouse bathroom so that nobody could see in. It didn't make sense out here, but she was grateful for it now. The windowsill was set so high she could stand in the tub and balance the gun on it. She could stand like this for hours without straining something.

It was totally quiet now. She heard a car driving somewhere. It had to be far off. The wind carried sound. She could never live out here, in an area where cell phones couldn't function reliably. Jayne wondered which cable you'd have to slice through or which pole you'd have to chop down to take out the landline as well.

AUGUST 24, 7:40 PM

The large number of cars inside the fence baffled Gcilitshana. Had they all been parked there when the first shots were fired? He could see his car, which was sitting on the south side. But that little Daimler...He didn't recall seeing it before. It had to belong to that skinny white woman. The only one beyond the fence was the Quick Trans van.

He could also see the fat seed rep. *If it weren't so noisy around here*, the cop thought, *the vultures would already be hard at work.*

He'd gotten the easiest job of all. Here on the side with the farm gate. Nothing had happened out here yet. Maybe this side of the house seemed the least vulnerable. Why should they change their strategy? Whoever they were.

What they were experiencing here wouldn't fit into any criminal statistic. The shooters obviously weren't interested in just hastily grabbing whatever might fit into their pockets during an attack. Quick inside the house, violence if necessary, and off with the haul. Their goal was apparently not to kill as many people as possible, either. They could've already done that. If they hadn't started their attack from so far away, everyone who'd been outside at the time would be dead by now. What was he missing?

The road that led from the gate toward King ran straight and long. Despite the darkness, he could make out the pale surface. Nobody could cross it without him seeing them. He just had to stay alert.

He heard the maid cough out in the hallway. What was her name again?

AUGUST 24, 7:42 PM

If only he could see someone, but it was dark.

They would pay for what happened to Ma.

As soon as he saw somebody, Zak planned to fire. That much he knew. He would take care of them.

Dad's new gun, the one he'd recently bought. Zak could hardly believe he had let him use it. All you had to do was pull the trigger once, and the bullets would fire in a staccato blast.

As soon as something moved, he was going to do that. No doubt about it. Zak was so excited, he pulled the trigger, releasing a barrage of bullets into the night.

AUGUST 24, 7:40 PM

Thabo Buti was scared, but it was his duty to stand here. He was older than most of them. Sipho, Cesar and Jo-Jo had young children.

The Boss wouldn't give him a gun anyway. Muller wasn't exactly in a position to take over responsibility as things stood. Now that his wife was dead, the Boss was no longer the boss.

He gazed into the darkness. Most of the bullets had come from that direction, the ones that had destroyed the living room. That McKenzie was right. Six, seven people, that was it. What did they want? The Boss had just paid the workers, so there wasn't much cash around right now. Of course, he always had a few thousand rands on him, a small fortune. And people had been killed for just a few hundred. But to attack a farm for that? This country would eventually drive them all crazy. In some illegal bar, two people argued about some trivial thing, and then one of them pulled a knife and stabbed the other. Someone wanted another person's cell phone and shot a hole in the latter's head to get it. So why not attack farms for a few thousand rands? Considering all that.

He remembered the guns. But who else knew about them? The boss had so many stuck in his hiding place. He had only seen them twice in all the years. Guns were easy to sell. Just like cars. Besides the Mullers' vehicles, there were a few others in the compound. But who would have known they'd be here around lunchtime? And now most of them were shot up.

Money, guns, maybe cars, Thabo thought. As

soon as anything moved out there, he would fire.

It was surprisingly quiet in the house, which was why a story someone had told him once came to mind. It was about a tunnel that ran from the farmhouse to the nearest road. No idea if the story was true, but right now it would fit, considering how quiet it was right now.

The President had arranged for a bunker to be built under his property. Perhaps there was one here, too. They could burn down the house, and the farmers would survive on the provisions they had stored down there.

"What should we do?"

Kaiser had returned a few minutes ago. He had made the rounds. That was necessary now that they had spread themselves around the farmhouse. His voice was hoarse, as usual.

"We could storm the house!" Kaiser said.

"No, they'd just pick us off. We're safe here. We'll wait."

"How much longer?"

That was a good question. A very good one, to be honest. If they hadn't managed to kill anyone else, then the farmer and the young woman and the cop and the four blacks were inside the house. Seven people. Plus anyone they hadn't seen outdoors. He bet there were several of these. But maybe they had taken out a whole bunch of them already. If only he knew. If only they could see more.

He heard a shot from behind the house.

"Shit!" Kaiser said.

AUGUST 24, 7:42 PM

There was definitely at least one person stand-ing behind the large bush. But if she simply risked taking the shot and missed her target, then the people out there would be alarmed. Better to wait.

In the background, she heard one of the girls start crying again. Tramping on the stairs. They had agreed that those without guns would remain in the upstairs hallway.

Shots. From an automatic.

Jayne winced, losing her focus on the bush and its surroundings. However, she resisted the urge to see what had happened. The shots had come from inside the house.

It was quiet again.

She concentrated and relocated the big bush.

AUGUST 24, 7:45 PM

"Wait!" he held Kaiser back. "Tell the others to aim at the upstairs windows. And they should wait until they hear me fire. Got it? I'll start it off."

Kaiser grunted.

"And be careful when you move around. Obviously, they're armed in there!"

Kaiser set off.

AUGUST 24, 7:47 PM

There was movement behind the bush. This time she didn't just imagine it. She could almost see it. That was how well her eyes had gotten used to the darkness.

There might even be two people behind the shrub. Something was happening there. The shots must have made them nervous.

Now someone emerged. He headed toward the west. Not fast, but briskly. Slightly hunched over.

Jayne followed him. The figure vanished swiftly behind the next bush. She aimed her gun at the spot where she assumed the person would come back into view.

And then he reappeared. Jayne tightened her trigger finger and thought about Rosie Muller.

And fired.

Got him, she thought. *Like a springbok.*

AUGUST 24, 7:50 PM

The first thing he heard was a single shot. Cesar Mhlaba looked around. None of the others sitting beside him on the staircase looked startled. Nobody cried out. Too much had already happened this evening. Then another shot was fired. And then another.

A pause.

More silence. Still no one said anything. Trixie sighed quietly. She was sitting above him, holding her two girls.

And then all the pistols and guns in the world went off at once. Cesar ducked down, his head on his knees.

Above and underneath them, windowpanes exploded around the house. An automatic gun clattered. Bullets in stone and wood.

After a few seconds, the sound of splintering glass stopped. But the bullets continued to hail into the house. Cesar heard a dull thwackthwack-thwack as bullets lodged themselves into a wall somewhere over his head.

"Urrrr!" someone said. The sound came from below.

The sound of bullets grew thinner. Regardless of which guns these people were using, one thing was true for every one of them: they had to be reloaded.

"Sipho's been hit!" he heard Jo-Jo call in Xhosa. "Sipho! Sipho!"

Cesar leaped up, listening for noises in the distance. Only scattered shots.

He cautiously climbed up, step-by-step. Somewhere downstairs, individual shots were still landing. He saw Jo-Jo's silhouette bending over Sipho. Boss Muller stood beside them. He leaned down, gingerly running his hand across Sipho's head. He felt something liquid and warm.

"He's dead, brother!" Jo-Jo said.

Up above, Cesar heard the gun that had gone off earlier fire again. Rattattattattat. Rattattattattat. Rattattattat.

Then a "Ha!" followed. Cesar knew who that was.

AUGUST 24, 7:50 PM

Right before the first shot struck, Thabo Buti was thinking about Noluthando, his wife. And the families who lived beside them on the other side of the farm. Could they hear the shots from there? And what would they do? Cell phones worked just as unreliably over there as they did here. And they didn't have any other phones there.

Then the shot came. It had been quiet outside for a few minutes, and Thabo winced. He gathered his thoughts, and was trying to find something to shoot at when the second and third blasts came in quick succession. They weren't coming from the side of the house he was watching.

The echo from the third shot had not quite faded when all hell broke loose. Thabo dropped to the floor and almost let his gun fall out the window. It took a few seconds for him to hear the sound of bullets striking the outside wall of his room. It was more like he felt them, since he was leaning against the very wall they were hitting. He sank down a little more until he was practically lying on the floor. In the staircase, a bullet struck something hanging on the wall, knocking it to the floor. He didn't run the risk of seeing what it was.

Gradually, the constant shooting tapered off. Thabo was trembling all over.

A few individual shots came from somewhere, but Thabo had the feeling it was over now.

AUGUST 24, 7:56 PM

Zak could hear individual shots being fired from the other side of the house. It seemed to be over. For now. His window had been blasted away in the barrage of bullets. He had crawled under his bed as soon as it started. Now he crept back out and propped the new gun on the window frame. He stayed stretched out underneath it, but kept his finger on the trigger. He couldn't afford to misfire.

AUGUST 24, 7:56 PM

More rattattattat. And the scattered shots from the south side. Gcilitshana's wall had been spared most of the bullets. He suspected the few shots on his side had been intended for the front entrance area. But there were at least two people on his side. Did they want to shoot down the front door and storm the house?

He slowly raised his head and looked out the window. He was careful not to expose much more than the upper half of his head as he did so.

Nothing. Just darkness. And the road to King. How in the world would they get out of here? Outside help was the only solution. Maybe he could somehow get to his car. He hadn't been totally truthful. It actually might be possible to establish a radio connection from there. He had simply been unwilling to go outside. It would have been suicide.

It would still be suicide. Besides, the car had to be shot to pieces by now.

There was now movement out on the path. Gcilitshana caught sight of a figure behind a tree. The person was tall. He had the impression that the figure had glanced across at him and then crossed the path. There were a few trees close to the road and a bush next to them. But he could no longer see the figure.

He should have had his gun cocked. Then he would have definitely fired.

AUGUST 24, 7:58 PM

It had almost been a minute since the last shot.

Only one person is standing out there, Jayne thought. Only one left. She had hit the other one. But he had several guns out there. One shot had just crashed into the bathroom. The latest one.

Very cautiously, she peered through the window opening. Nothing. She pulled back again.

If they were actually all reloading right now, it might be a good opportunity to deliver another blow. Jayne inhaled deeply and raised her gun.

At first, all she saw was darkness.

Patience.

How were they communicating with each other out there? Not by cell phone, that much was clear. If they couldn't get a signal in here, then they didn't have one outside, either.

Slowly, she was able to make out the shapes outdoors. That large bush. She was so certain that someone was concealed behind it.

She swung her gun slowly to the right. Until she saw the guy she had just shot. Had she actually killed him? She was sure she had. He was stretched on the ground, unable to ever move again on his own. Six remaining. Or seven. At the most.

Back to her original target. Past the large bush and farther left. There were trees with boulders behind them, rising out of one of the potato fields. Nothing else. Just as she was about to return to the big bush, something moved.

A person!

Of course, Jayne thought. That was the only way they could communicate. Via messengers. There had to be a leader somewhere, the one giving orders. She tracked the figure. A tall man, wide-shouldered and heavy. However, he slipped confidently and nimbly from tree to tree, from bush to bush. Unlike the man she'd just killed, he dashed from one shadow to another. He had just reached the large bush.

It was now completely quiet. Jayne aimed carefully for the center of the bush and fired.

AUGUST 24, 7:57 PM

It was a matter in which he was heavily invested. He fired one more time. He had to reload, anyway.

They all had to reload, which was why the shooting had stopped.

This was his biggest investment to date. However, this also involved a considerable score. Over the past year, he had started reading financial magazines. And he had immediately been taken with the language. For the first time, he felt understood. He was an entrepreneur. A plan was part of every good business venture. A plan and a sufficient amount of money to help you get things off the ground. Personnel also belonged to the financial considerations. A spaza shop didn't require a large staff, just a single person who could sell goods through a barred window. It only took one person, not two, to wash a car. And here, according to his calculations, it had been advisable to show up with six hired people.

Admittedly, things were supposed to have run very differently. And now, he was down to five men. And it was getting colder. August on the Eastern Cape was frigging cold.

A sound from close by. The guy that Kaiser had dragged along. What was his name? A cousin.

"Chief," he said. "Shouldn't we change something?"

"Change what?"

"I don't know. You're the one with the plan!"

He nodded, although he knew the other man could hardly see him. And he heard the shot as it fired. He grabbed for the cousin and pulled him to the ground. Something crashed through the bush.

From the dirt, he asked: "Everything alright?"

"Yeah." The cousin shook himself free. "Who's inside that house?"

He considered briefly and wished he had an answer. But had to admit that he didn't have one.

AUGUST 24, 7:59 PM

Another single shot was fired. Thabo Buti suspected that it hadn't come from outside, but from inside the house.

Then silence. He listened and noticed that it wasn't completely silent. Two birds were chirping to each other. A breeze seemed to be blowing outside. Someone was whimpering. It was a masculine voice, which was also coming from outside.

He got to his feet and stretched his stiff leg before opening the door to the staircase. He recognized Jo-Jo's voice.

Thabo's eyes struggled to adjust to the darkness. There was no moonlight in this area. "What's going on, Boss?"

"Sipho," he heard Muller say. "Sipho's dead."

Thabo's stomach lurched. Sipho was one of the good ones. A young wife and two children. Even after a long workday, he always had a ready sentence that could make you laugh. A man who came out alright where life was concerned.

Had come out. Thabo went down the stairs. "We have to do something, Boss," he said.

"Yeah."

AUGUST 24, 8:01 PM

"We have to do something, Boss." That was probably the foreman's voice.

"Yeah." That had been Franz, Jayne was sure of that.

She was standing at the top of the stairs and could feel the children trembling beside her. Trixie was humming a barely audible, monotonous melody to try to calm them. Down the stairs, a man was weeping. A door opened behind her, and a little farther away, another one swung open.

"I showed them!" Zak said.

Rosie should've spent less time worrying about Jesus and more time on Zak, Jayne thought. Jesus was always close at hand, but Zak had somehow never managed to get his act together.

"I definitely got one of them!" he now said.

"They're using a courier!" another voice on the same floor said. The policeman. "They can't call anyone, either. That's why they have to send someone around to coordinate the attacks."

"I took out one of them," Jayne said. "I'm sure of that!"

Murmuring on the stairs.

"What can we do now?" Trixie.

"I'm going out and taking care of this, once and for all!" Franz.

"Dad, don't say that." Trixie. "You can't do that."

AUGUST 24, 8:03 PM

Betsie stood up from her spot on the stairs. She had been sitting only a short distance above Sipho. She could have just as easily been the one hit.

Nobody here was going to listen to her, which meant she could go brew some coffee. That didn't require any light, and they could all use a hot drink. It was winter, after all, and the temperature would just keep dropping.

Vuyo must've driven to Ginsberg. Home. It was just strange he hadn't said anything.

As she filled the electric kettle with water, Betsie's eyes filled with tears. Would she still be needed on the farm now that Rosie was dead? She set the canister on its stand, pressed the red button, and wiped her face.

"Let's take them by surprise!" Zak cried from somewhere.

"Idiot!" she heard Boss Muller say. She closed the kitchen door.

Betsie pulled her phone out of her smock. She walked up and down the gigantic kitchen. Nothing. If only she could talk to Vuyo.

God, how she loved that child!

Sure, the boy had made mistakes. The attack on the telephone kiosk in Duncan Village had been wrong. But Vuyo had said he hadn't been the one who fired the gun. At least, nobody had been killed.

Not like what happened during the burglary in Gonubie. But Vuyo had said that all he did was stand guard for that one. And they had agreed that no one would get hurt. But something had gone wrong. At the trial, Vuyo had been sentenced to jail. Two years. He had been released on parole after a little over a year served.

But he was a good boy. Betsie poured the hot water into the coffee pot. Slowly, so the aroma could spread quickly. She then fetched the large tray, and filled it with cups as well as milk and sugar.

She heard a dog barking outside. Far away. It couldn't be one of theirs. They were dead.

AUGUST 24, 8:02 PM

It took a few minutes until he risked getting up off the ground. Kaiser's cousin had rolled himself up beside him. He poked him in the side. "Come on!"

Obviously, the people inside were well-trained. There was something going on here after all. It was just odd that they hadn't seen them when they started their attack. But they had been inside. Sharpshooters. Ex-military. Probably white men, between the ages of fifty and sixty, who had already killed a lot of black folks. They couldn't be too careful at this point.

If only he could call that damn doctor. Ramesh. Sleazy, like all Indians.

On the other hand, his other tips had resulted in good outcomes. He'd been a good business partner until now.

Ramesh made a good profit off his tips. "Thirty percent," he always said. And thirty percent was what he got, too. Usually.

One time, when he'd given Ramesh less than that, he had laid awake at night and wondered if the Indian had just been testing him.

Ramesh! With his medical practice. Where practically nobody went.

AUGUST 24, 8:07 PM

Gcilitshana was still carrying his gun as he slowly felt his way down the stairs. Cesar and Jo-Jo were hauling the dead Sipho into the downstairs bathroom, and Betsie had just emerged from the kitchen with a tray. He could now see quite well in the darkness. Betsie stopped in the middle of the hallway.

"Just leave it on the floor," he said to her, as he rested his hand on Franz Muller's shoulder. He squeezed it quickly, filled two cups with coffee, and stepped into the living room.

It took at least a minute for the farmer to follow him. Gcilitshana could see his silhouette on the threshold between the corridor and the living room.

"Over here," he said. "In the corner!"

It occurred to him that he wasn't sitting far from the bloodstain that documented Rosie Muller's end. Nonetheless, the farmer moved toward him, accepting the warm cup before joining him on the floor.

Gcilitshana heard Muller sipping. He kept setting down his cup and breathing rapidly.

"Sir," Gcilitshana said. "I'm so sorry about what happened to your wife. Whatever happens here, assuming we make it, we'll bring the culprits to justice. I promise you that."

Muller drained his cup and grunted. "Yeah, yeah." He put his cup aside. "But what should we do to survive all this?"

Both fell silent. It was growing darker in the room. A cloud scudded across the moon. Gcilitshana also emptied his cup.

Footsteps drew closer out in the hallway, but nobody came into the living room.

"What do they want, anyway?" Gcilitshana asked.

"I don't know!"

"But...it has to be something!"

"Of course, it's something," Muller's voice sank. He was now the opposite of the white farmer that Gcilitshana had known before now. All assertiveness, every bit of dominance and arrogance, was now gone. He suddenly felt sorry for Muller. "Of course, it's something," Muller repeated. "They want to take whatever they can get."

"Hmm...But you can't mean that this is a typical farm attack. And..." He didn't want to ask the question, but he couldn't help it. "Who are they?"

"You know very well who they are!" Muller didn't grow louder, but his tone sharpened. "You know exactly how many farmers have been murdered over the past few years."

"Across this entire country," he added after a pause.

Gcilitshana saw a shadow in the hall and thought perhaps he was needed there. But he couldn't leave yet.

"Once they've murdered the last farmer, they'll see that they can't eat money. But as long as the police falsify the farm murder statistics..."

"We aren't falsifying anything. We're just not releasing them anymore."

"But that's the same thing!" Now louder.

The shadow now moved into the living room. "There's no point to all this! If we want to get out of here alive, we have to do something."

"Jayne," Muller said. "I don't understand what you want! Should we go out there?"

"Yes. We have no other choice!"

Gcilitshana wished he could see Muller's expression, but it was too dark for that. Instead, he said, "You're right. In theory, we have to go out."

"Yeah, sure," Muller said. "In theory! But how do we manage that? They're waiting for us out there. Your people!"

"Don't be ridiculous, Franz!"

"But those are black people out there!"

"That's obvious," Jayne said. "They outnumber us and have less money than we do. We don't need to argue about that. And now let's pull ourselves together and consider what we can do to get out of this alive."

She's not half-bad at this, Gcilitshana thought.

She wasn't even a little hysterical. Knew how to wait until an opportunity arose. Like now.

"What do you think, Mrs. McKenzie?" he asked. "How can we get out of here?" He hesitated. "That's what you want, right? For us to go out."

"Nonsense!" Muller.

"Yes. We have to."

"How?"

"We can go out the bathroom window."

"Where the bodies are?"

"Uh-huh!"

"Why?"

"Because there's ivy growing on that side of the house. The wall along there is dark. They won't be able to see us right away. We'll have to climb out and then move along the ground. And there's a spot along the fence that hasn't been completely cleared. There are some apple trees there. That's where we need to go."

"And then?"

"We have to get out, away from the farmyard. We'll cut a hole in the fence and then hunt them down."

Gcilitshana had never met a woman like this. Many of the new hires in the police department were young women, but they weren't like this.

"What do you mean 'hunt'?" he asked.

"What do you think?" she shot back.

AUGUST 24, 8:07 PM

Thabo had wrapped his arms around Jo-Jo. The boy could no longer stay calm and was sobbing. He was clinging to Thabo like a small child.

"What are we going to do now?" he asked. Thabo knew he should have a ready answer. He was the older one. But he didn't.

The young repairman was taking care of the delivery guy. Cesar was sitting next to him, staring into the darkness. Trixie was up on the stairs with her children. She had figured out the safest spot, the one where the bullets were the least likely to reach. Zak was stalking around upstairs, at least that was what it sounded like to Thabo. Betsie had disappeared back into the kitchen. She might feel the safest in there. If the shooting started up again, she would have to either hide in there or make her way down the dangerous hallway, where the windows had already been shot out.

Mrs. Muller and Sipho were lying in the bathroom. She in the bathtub, he beside it. Even in death, she had it better. *If we get out of this alive, I'll need to go to Sipho's family*, Thabo thought. He could try to comfort Jo-Jo. He could just as well leave it be, too.

The Boss now stepped out of the living room, along with Mrs. McKenzie and the policeman. Somehow, the Boss didn't look as if he had made any decisions in there. He preceded the two others, but the woman and Gcilitshana looked like they were wrapping up whatever decision they had made without Muller's involvement. However, Thabo could see how the Boss was stretching, trying to see who all was sitting on the stairs.

"Zak," he called. "Where are you? Come down here. We need to talk." He then looked in Thabo's direction. "Thabo, where's Betsie?"

The maid came out of the kitchen with another tray. Sandwiches and cake. Nobody had eaten supper. Everyone helped themselves. The repair guy took two sandwiches and gave one to the messenger.

With his mouth full, the cop cleared his throat. Cesar, who always knew everything, had heard that Gcilitshana took bribes. From anyone. He allegedly had helped cook up plans with several cattle thieves, advising them on how they could most easily steal animals. He also took money from farms in exchange for offering them protection. Last week, Thabo had run into Cesar one night, when they had both been unable to fall asleep. They had sat in front of Cesar's small house and talked. And Cesar had said that he had heard that Gcilitshana had once shot two people over a disagreement. Over a few hundred rands. Thabo remembered hearing something about this on the radio. About people who had been found dead in the street. The police had said that they were searching for a motive for the murder. And for the murderer, of course.

"We..." the policeman was now saying. "We've decided that we have to do something."

"Exactly," Zak shouted.

"Shut up!" the Boss said.

Gcilitshana continued. "We can wait here until something else happens or they come in here to shoot us one by one. Or we can go out." That was obviously the end of his speech. He glanced at the Boss, who was watching Mrs. McKenzie.

And she then explained how things would go.

Thabo had never seen a woman like this.

AUGUST 24, 8:18 PM

On the one hand, they needed a new strategy. But on the other hand, he needed to figure out more about the people inside the farmhouse. But only God knew how long it would be until he had a cell phone signal. He could climb into the car they had hidden behind the hedge. Drive a few kilometers. But on his way there, he might easily pick up a few stray bullets.

He had to speak with the doctor.

"Pay attention," he said to Kaiser's cousin, who was still crouched next to him. He suddenly realized that the cousin didn't know about Kaiser's death yet. "You need to make the rounds now. Go back the way you came. Tell everyone to wait. But if anyone leaves the house, they should open fire. Got it?"

"Yeah," the cousin said.

"And come back along the same way. You'll almost make it around the house, but retrace your route." He gestured to show what he meant.

The cousin watched and nodded.

"I think it's too dangerous over there." He pointed in the direction where Kaiser had disappeared. "Now go. And tell them that we'll fire again once I give them the sign."

When the cousin returned, he would try to call.

AUGUST 24, 8:16 PM

"Stay here," Franz said. Jayne had heard this tone used frequently with Zak. No dissent allowed.

"If someone needs to stay here...I mean...
Someone has to protect the women and children."

The cop wants to abandon us. Nice try, she
thought. If they ended up actually killing someone, it would be good to have an officer close by.
He would vouch for them.

"Zak knows his way around guns," Franz now
said. "I want him to stay here." Jayne hadn't seen
him this decisive since Rosie's death.

"I can go," Thabo said, raising his hand.

"No, you can't," Franz said. "Not with your leg."

"Boss, I can run faster than you!"

"You're staying here!"

Jayne didn't contradict him. Going out with
Franz and the cop was the best solution. Here
inside the house, Thabo could keep Zak in
check if he snapped. Now all she had to do was
address one last delicate matter. "We all have to
be armed," she said.

"Absolutely not!" Franz.

"That's crazy!" Zak.

"Boss, what if you don't come back?" Thabo.

"Wouldn't that make you happy! You're armed,
and so is Zak."

"What about me? I could stay here!" The cop.

Whether in the church or in other places, Jayne
gladly let others steer conversations. And at home,
Arnold had always been the one who laid down
the law. But now she had to intervene. "Be quiet,
all of you! And listen."

Everyone stopped talking. Everyone listened.
She was surprised.

"Thabo's right. There is a chance we won't be

coming back. Hopefully, God will prevent that, but other situations might arise in which everyone here in the house would need to be armed. We're going to cut a hole in the fence and leave the yard area. If something were to happen, we might not get back quickly enough to protect all of you." She paused and wished she could see the others' faces. "Which of you can even shoot?"

Murmuring. Agreement.

"I can't!" That was Betsie's voice.

"Franz," Jayne said. "If we don't do this, we can't go out there."

"But..." Zak couldn't think of any arguments against this, because there actually weren't any.

"Come on, Franz. Let's go gather them up," Jayne said.

The farmer took a deep breath. "Come on, Zak!"

AUGUST 24, 8:39 PM

This was precisely the situation his oldest son Pat had always warned him about. "Dad, one day they'll come to get you. They'll be standing at your door, and you'll remember what I always said."

Muller pulled the threadbare oriental rug in his office to the side.

People never talked about who THEY actually were. Everyone knew without saying. Now "they" were here.

He stood up. "You do it, Zak!"

His son knelt down, and unfastened the door set into the floor. Not particularly secure, but who ever looked under a rug?

"Dad," he said, as he slowly lifted both door panels. "I think that we're making a mistake here. The workers shouldn't be armed. They have no idea how to work these things."

"They're used to defending their families," Jayne said from where she had sat down behind the desk. "My God, I'm exhausted!"

Muller watched her prop her head in her hands. He was amazed by her energy. He had hardly registered her since Arnold's death. She had occasionally visited Rosie. That was it.

Thirty-eight years, he thought. *And now... they're here.*

"Do it, Zak. They should take up posts around the house and keep watch. Thabo will lead them. That's what he does anyway. And you, Zak..." Muller tugged the rug back in front of the desk, panting slightly. "Stay vigilant!"

AUGUST 24, 8:52 PM

They were forcing him. He was only here because of a stupid coincidence. Because of Roelf Botha. Because of his cancer. But what could he do? The people expected him to go out with them. Gcilitshana opened the door and peered into the bathroom. He knew what he would see and was relieved it was so dark. Nonetheless, a little moonlight had worked its way inside through the shot-out window. The dark stuff underneath Rosie Muller's head was her blood. It contrasted sharply with the white bathtub. The worker had also bled out more since they had put him under the sink.

"Keep going!" Muller urged from behind.

"Good luck!" someone farther away said. That had to be the foreman.

Gcilitshana reached across the bathtub and opened the window. The farmer had insisted that they draw straws to see who went out the window first. He had lost.

"You won!" Muller had said.

McKenzie had pulled off her blue jeans. She was wearing long black leggings underneath them. Combined with her black blouse, it took only a few seconds for her to be perfectly clothed for their excursion. Muller had needed to change clothes. Black jeans and a navy blue shirt.

And he was wearing his blue uniform. He wished he had something more comfortable on, but the uniform also had its perks. Even the most hardened tsotsis preferred not to shoot a cop. They knew what the consequences were. Not just for themselves, but for others. Raids, roadblocks, deaths on the other side.

He climbed onto the edge of the bathtub. Wiped the shards of glass away. As he cautiously stuck his head out the window, a cold wind wrapped itself around his nose. Below, the lawn, probably a little damp. He wondered momentarily if he should turn around and go out feet first, but he saw himself stuck in the window with a bullet in his back. Not a pretty thought. So he dove down and landed in the grass on all fours. He flattened himself against the ground and waited. They had agreed that McKenzie would count to fifty before she followed him.

AUGUST 24, 8:54 PM

It was obvious he didn't want to go outside. The cop. Would have preferred to defend the people inside.

Now, he jumped out the window, as stiff as an old dog. Jayne hoped that the splashing sound the grass made when he hit the ground wasn't audible on the other side of the fence. And that he hadn't broken anything.

As soon as he landed, she climbed up on the tub and stood on the edge. She had taken the automatic away from Zak because she might need it more urgently outside than the people remaining indoors. She started to count.

Gcilitshana was flattened against the grass like a cockroach on a kitchen floor. Jayne scanned the area behind him. It was astonishing how quickly your eyes could adjust to altered conditions. She had a clear view through the darkness of whatever might be happening beyond the fence. Except for a few trees, everything had been cut low for a radius of fifty meters. This was good if you wanted to see well. And bad if you didn't want to be seen.

All that still remained was a small group of about a dozen apple trees. And this was where they wanted to cut the hole in the fence. Worst case scenario: This was right where the tsotsis were hiding. However, the only thing you could see from that spot was the corner of the farmhouse. And the gunfire had definitely come from a different angle. That's what she thought, anyway. If they encountered them at the trees, they'd end up in a deadly shootout.

"Do you see anything?" Franz asked quietly.

"No!" If they were over there, then they had something better to do than watch this side of the farmhouse. Maybe they were talking among themselves.

Jayne handed Franz her gun and pushed herself up on the windowsill. She turned around and faced the house as she slid to the ground.

AUGUST 24, 8:53 PM

The cousin was back.

"Where's Kaiser?" he asked. He accepted a shrug as an answer, but that wouldn't suffice for the entire night.

"Everyone's taking it easy," he then said. "But when it's time, they'll be a hundred percent up and going."

"Okay. Just stay here. Only shoot if you see something. I also want to make the rounds. A little farther around the house. Have to think about how we can get things moving again."

"Sure!"

With that, he trudged off across the adjacent field. The next settlement had to be in this direction. He didn't know this area all that well. He was more of a city guy, but he remembered seeing a small village somewhere over here. And where there were houses, there was a cell phone signal.

He was ruining his shoes. The dust was fine. You could get rid of that. But the dirt stuck like crazy to shoes. He had no choice in the matter.

Everything had been so clear cut this afternoon. He still wasn't sure what had gone wrong.

There were obviously too many people around. The cop also hadn't been part of the plan. The security personnel inside also didn't make sense.

Still no bars.

AUGUST 24, 7:54 PM

Dan van der West enjoyed this part of the day. He liked going to bed early.

He usually lay awake for a little while, thinking about things, before falling asleep eventually.

All the normal boxes had been checked off along his journey to slumber, but then something caught his attention. He had spent his entire life on this farm, all forty-nine years of it. And he knew every noise and every gust of wind, every chord that could be created by humans, animals and nature.

Something was off.

He sat up and listened.

If he was honest with himself, he would have to admit that he had just heard gunfire. He knew that sound quite well. He had been in the army. Happily so. It had served a good purpose. He had learned to use guns, something that was always useful.

Gunfire was unusual. Especially in the middle of the night. But where was it coming from? He listened harder. There it was again. Right?

Van der West stood up and got dressed. Shirt, shorts, socks, and thick shoes. The same, regardless of the season. Since his wife Marietta had started taking care of her mother in Port Elizabeth and was gone more than she was home, nobody saw him anyway. Marietta had always said he should change his clothes every day. Had she planned to call again today?

He stood quietly outside his front door and listened. Nothing.

The wind was coming from...the north. Which farm was the closest? Several. And to the north? Muller. Dan van der West went back inside his house, grabbed his hunting rifle from the gun cabinet, and locked the front door. He then unlocked the massive padlock on the gate in the fence that surrounded his farmhouse and relocked it after he stepped through it. He gave the lock a tug to verify it had caught and set off northward on foot.

AUGUST 24, 8:58 PM

Jayne and Gcilitshana were lying in the grass, just as still as Rosie beneath him. Franz Muller refused to look down. Into the tub on the edge of which he was now standing.

He felt tears trickle down his cheeks. *Crying*, he thought. *I haven't done that since I was a child. Pull yourself together, Franz. You are the master of the house. The Boss.*

Nobody was moving outside. At least, no one that he could see. If he remained silent, Jayne would stand up and take the guns. She was already moving a little.

He handed her the gun that Zak had been using. She had insisted on taking it with her. Gcilitshana had his service weapon, and he was supposed to get another pistol as well. Lastly, he handed Jayne the two pistols with which, she said, she wanted to go hunting. That sounded obscene somehow.

He then sat on the windowsill and threw one last glance at his dead Rosie. And then lowered himself. He scraped both elbows on the wall and took a section of the ivy down with him.

Hopefully, they hadn't seen anything.

AUGUST 24, 9:01 PM

Thabo Buti was now in Zak's room. The Boss had insisted that he keep watch from here.

Zak had been angry. "That's my room!"

"It doesn't matter," the Boss had said. "Not at all. You go into the girls' room. You'll have to defend us from there soon enough."

At the moment, Thabo was watching as the Boss dropped onto the grass. *He had caught himself*, Thabo thought. But there was something else at stake. Not just a number of lives, but also his position, his honor. Always trying to maintain his stance, Franz Muller. *This new role actually suited him quite well*, Thabo thought. The pastor of his church called it humility.

All three of them were now lying there, like lions getting ready to stalk their prey.

AUGUST 24, 9:07 PM

He wasn't used to walking. Especially not over plowed fields. Normally, he would have driven his car. It was wintertime, fortunately. Not much was growing out here. And he was lucky that it wasn't so damp that he sank into the dirt with each step.

But this was still enough.

This was the boundary between the farm where they were and the neighboring one. He had scouted out the terrain a little, two days ago. Everywhere there were signs explaining which corn varieties would soon be growing here. The signs also said that the corn belonged to some company.

How could corn belong to a company? It belonged to the farmers who cultivated it. That was exactly the problem in South Africa. The ground belonged to the whites. Still did. Regardless of what had happened.

And still no bars.

AUGUST 24, 9:14 PM

Van der West made a large arc around Muller's farmhouse. Nothing. Total silence.

He then sat down underneath a bush and waited. Eyes and ears on standby. The military was the best school one could dream of. Besides humility, one thing above all else was taught there: patience.

He was already starting to feel cold when he saw the figure trudging across the field, mumbling to himself. Nothing comprehensible. He spoke Xhosa quite fluently, but the mumbling was abstract. A muted production of sounds.

A young black man.

Maybe no longer quite so young.

He was plodding across the field as if worried he might get his shoes dirty. City boy.

He was holding something that he then glanced at. A phone. Van der West saw the glow of the screen in the darkness. More mumbling.

He let the guy move on. It was flat right around here. Regardless of how dark it was, he wouldn't lose him. Besides, this was his terrain.

AUGUST 24, 9:11 PM

"Sssst!" McKenzie hissed before crawling toward the trees.

Gcilitshana followed and heard Muller coming behind him. They moved slowly so they wouldn't make noise or stir up any dust. She had insisted on that.

When she reached the first tree, McKenzie stopped and gestured that they should stay down. The trees weren't very large. A township boy could have hidden behind one of them. An ANC politician couldn't have.

Gcilitshana thought back through the strategy McKenzie had laid out. Slowly to the fence, then cut the hole. Out and decide in which direction to go. Together.

Five trees on this side of the fence, possibly twice as many on the other side. She now stood up. Muller and he remained on their stomachs. McKenzie was no fatter than a township boy. A runner, he'd bet.

She waited a minute, leaning against a tree before moving to the fence. He heard the high-pitched clang that came when you cut through wire. She returned to the tree. And waited.

AUGUST 24, 9:21 PM

Clouds scudded across the sky as the darkness

grew even darker. For a split second, a single bar appeared on his screen. But as soon as he stopped to dial, it was gone. How could anyone live out here?

He walked slowly on. It couldn't take much longer. Ramesh had forgotten to tell him something. He had definitely forgotten something.

Besides, he needed to get back to the others. You couldn't leave them on their own for too long. First of all, they only knew what they absolutely needed to know. And secondly, some of them he didn't even trust an inch.

And thirdly, Kaiser was dead, and he was the only one who knew that. Hopefully, none of the others had stumbled across him.

And fourthly...He had no idea how long the guy had been on his heels. A white man in shorts. A farmer probably, but not someone who had anything to do with the people in the house.

What was he up to out here? Farmers got up really early, which meant they went to bed early. This was definitely the wrong time for him to be out.

The farmer was darting from tree to tree and bush to bush. He had probably learned that in the army. But there was one place that taught you even more about life. And that was jail.

Two bars on his screen. Now was the time to call the doctor. He held the screen so that it would keep glowing. The farmer should be able to see it clearly enough.

AUGUST 24, 9:15 PM

Jayne was already through the fence. She was once again positioned so that she was practically invisible. *She's really skinny*, Muller thought. All that exercise she did. Since Arnold's death, she had started jogging through Beacon Bay in the mornings. Ten kilometers, she said. He had caught sight of her once from his car when on his way to an appointment in East London. In leggings and top, all skin and bones. He had wondered how someone her age could stay so fit.

"Sssst!"

Gcilitshana crawled toward the fence. Jayne had cut it so that they could only get through it on their hands and knees. And she had chosen a spot located between two trees. If you were on the other side, you probably wouldn't be able to see the hole unless you were standing right on top of it.

Muller dragged himself slowly toward the fence.

The cop was already leaning against a tree on the other side of it.

"What do we do now? Do we want to get away from this spot?" Muller heard him ask.

The farmer's shirt got snagged on the wire as he pulled himself through the opening. In the silence, he heard it rip.

"Yes." Jayne.

"But first we have to get our bearings. Look. Listen."

"Then be quiet!"

Muller saw the policeman's shoes and took up

a position behind the next tree. He had left the apple trees standing when he had cleared the ring around the farmhouse years ago. Because they produced a good yield. This might doubly prove the wisdom of his decision. "What should we do now, Jayne?"

"What Mr. Gcilitshana suggested," she said very quietly. "Look and listen."

Muller understood what she meant, but there wasn't much to hear. Well...at least, no more than usual. A grasshopper struggling to survive the winter. The wind. Not much more. So he concentrated on seeing. He stared to the north.

His eyes were still good, despite the fact he now needed reading glasses. However, he didn't see much more than the ornamental bushes that separated the field they had planted in carrots from the one they had sown in potatoes. Shots had also come from over there. From somewhere over there. They had smashed into one of the living room windows.

Was this also where the bullet that hit Rosie had come from?

The line of bushes waved in concert with the wind, which was coming from somewhere inland. A little too warm for this time of year. But it was still wintry cold. Swaying gently in one direction, then in the other. Nothing suspicious.

Maybe they had already moved on. But to where?

Why had they even come out here? And what were Jayne and the cop seeing?

More movement. The bushes were almost as

tall as a man. Muller noticed that the one on the edge of the cleared area was no longer moving. Behind it, the wind was still doing its job. He could see that very clearly. Back and forth, very gently. Back and forth. Back and forth. The bush standing the closest to him was the only one not moving. That meant that someone was hiding behind it. Right in the middle of it. Or up against it.

Suddenly a hand descended on his shoulder, and Muller gave a start.

"Pssst!" Jayne.

Muller pointed toward the bushes.

"Yeah, I know!" she said.

"What should we do? Do you want to go over?"

"I'm going to shoot."

"From here?"

"Yeah."

"And then?"

"There'll be one fewer of them," she replied.

"Yes, but then?"

"I don't know. We'll have to see."

AUGUST 24, 9:34 PM

The city boy was clearly looking for a spot to make a call. Van der West could have shown him the places where there was always reception. It was hard out here, but possible.

The screen had stayed burning in the tsotsi's hand for a whole minute. The gunfire, this guy moving around close to his farm, the attempts to make a call. What was going on here? Had the tsotsi killed one of his neighbors and was now uncertain how to get back? To the road? To his car? But was he on the move all alone? Was he looking for the next farm? No, he was too poorly oriented for that. He must have come out here when it was light, and the darkness was affecting him more than he had thought it would.

He might have come with others, who were already dead. Farmers around here were vigilant. And prepared to kill.

Where had he gone? Van der West hadn't seen the glow for the past few minutes. The land sloped slightly uphill, which was the best spot for getting a cell phone signal. Maybe the other man had come to the same conclusion, regardless of his urban status.

He should be able to catch the tsotsi's trail again behind the three large boulders up there, the ones that had such an amazing view of the Amathole Mountains when it was light.

AUGUST 24, 9:33 PM

"What about the cop?" Muller asked. He glanced around, and Jayne followed his gaze.

"Do I need to ask his permission? We're here to defend ourselves, after all."

She hoisted her gun, but couldn't see anything through the scope. She lowered it and got her bearings. Maybe seventy or eighty meters. She just needed to find the front line of the bushes. She tried again.

It took about thirty seconds for her to locate the green plant, which looked gray in the dark- ness. A shade of gray that didn't stand out much from the other gray tones. But she had finally sighted the bush. Anyone who wasn't completely blind should have seen it instantly. Someone was hiding there. In theory, it could have also been a large animal, but where would it have come from? In the middle of this agricultural area.

She would need to shoot more than once. Child's play with this gun. Ideally straight across from a rise in order not to miss the person. Or could it possibly be two of them?

And then what? From where she was standing, she couldn't see the open spaces to either the west or the east. What would happen once she fired?

There are three possibilities, she thought.

Nothing would happen. Unlikely.

Those attackers that could would open fire on the house. Very likely.

Whoever was standing to the west and to the east—and perhaps anyone behind the bush who survived her bullets—would start shooting at them. For that, they first would need to orient themselves and figure out what had happened. A gun with a silencer would be ideal. The cop had brought one along out of the house, but they were too far away from her target or targets. A silencer was most suitable for close quarters.

She now found herself in a situation that more closely resembled her hunting experiences. It wasn't about speed, but about the right moment. And about precision. Shoot to kill. Not to injure, but to kill.

A plane flew overhead. Jayne had to resist the temptation to look up. It sounded like a large jet.

A late passenger flight on its way to the airport in East London.

She kept her eyes trained on the bush. As soon as the noise receded, she fired. Pop, pop, pop, pop, pop. Five times. The bush shook as if someone had grabbed onto it.

AUGUST 24, 9:48 PM

These three boulders suited him. Grouped together, they were as large as the bakery delivery van he had driven years ago. Before he had shifted professional gears. He walked around them once and saw the silhouette of the white man slowly approach. His movements weren't even slightly cautious. The farmer was moving as if he were on his own land.

Which you stole from us, he thought.

The white man drew closer. He was holding a hunting rifle. So that was how he visualized himself. First, figure out what is going on and then, shoot him in the back.

The white man was now walking straight toward him.

The farmer then hesitated, altered his direction, and walked around the boulders the same way Bulelani had done. Of course. He was searching. Bulelani wanted to see the light from his screen again. Preferably from a safe distance.

He pressed his body against the cold boulder and waited for the farmer to emerge on the other side of the stones. But he didn't come. Didn't he want to see if his quarry was hiding up here? It could be a trap. The farmer might be waiting for him at the other end of the rock formation, his rifle cocked and ready. Or...No, he wasn't calculating on someone hiding up in front of him. Why would he? He would have had to be discovered in that case. And the farmer was certain that hadn't happened.

Bulelani waited a few seconds before slipping around the other side of the boulders behind the farmer. Step by step. The ground was soft, and he didn't make a sound. A plane approached, filling the silence with noise. He pressed himself back against the stone and slowly rounded the next corner when the roar was directly above him.

And then he saw the white man. He was standing with his back to him, gazing up into the sky. This was an invitation he couldn't pass up. He reached into his left back pocket and pulled out the knife he hadn't intended to use today. He had even briefly considered leaving it at home. What luck.

With practiced ease, he flicked it open and crept cautiously toward the farmer. The jet had already passed, and the white man was lowering his head. But there was no going back now. He lifted his right arm and started to bend it to strike. Only one meter to go.

Then shots rang out. Far off.

The farmer turned around and unknowingly slipped out of his line of attack. At the same moment, the farmer swung the gun into his abdomen as he pivoted. Also unawares. The white man had been completely oblivious to the situation in which he was caught. As the pressure in his abdomen lessened, he rammed the knife into the farmer's body. Pulled it back out and struck again. And then into the back of the man doubled over in pain, whose anguish prevented him from crying out. In the back again and again and again. And then in the neck and the back of his head. The knife was sharp. Very sharp. It didn't take long for the other man to collapse onto the ground.

He kicked the dead man. His shoes were dirty, anyway.

Then he took off at a run. In the direction from which the shots had come. In the direction of the farm.

It took a few seconds for him to remember why he was even out here. He had needed to make a call.

AUGUST 24, 9:54 PM

The angle was lousy. Zak was practically stretched out across the windowsill. The old rifle with which he had learned to hunt was balanced on his outstretched left arm.

The shots had just died away. He had almost tumbled out the window when the gunfire began. Five or six shots. Had they actually found someone and taken him out? The shots had come from the small grove of trees where Dad was with Jayne and that black cop.

What was going to happen now? Had anybody been hit? Batshit crazy. That's what the idea to go out there had been.

AUGUST 24, 9:54 PM

He had easily opened the door, and now he

was peering out. No one was upstairs. They had all gathered on the staircase. Cesar didn't want to miss the opportunity.

The tsotsis could start shooting at any time. And the young Mr. Muller would fire back, but only until he caught a bullet himself. Cesar was holding the gun. He knew how to fire it. That was enough.

AUGUST 24, 9:53 PM

Bam, bam, bam, bam, bam. From where he was standing, Thabo had a good view of the scene. He had seen how the Boss, McKenzie and the cop had crawled to the fence and hidden behind the trees. McKenzie had eventually joined the Boss. And then he had seen her take aim.

She had taken a very, very long time before firing. But then everything went really fast. And now it was so quiet, as it always was when something happened and people needed time to process it.

McKenzie had fired at the row of bushes that separated the bare potato and carrot fields. He was now searching for any evidence that she had hit her target. If only he could find the spot.

There! That might be a person dragging someone else. Away from the house and the open area. And also away from his field of vision. Two people. One dead or injured, the other alive or at least not dead yet.

If one of them had been hit and if McKenzie had actually killed another one, then perhaps things weren't all that bleak after all. What had they estimated? That between six and eight attackers were involved. If two of the attackers were now knocked out, that constituted a major weakening. But of course, nobody on their side knew what the attackers plans were, how they were armed, or how they would react to the loss of their people. Thabo reshouldered his gun. He wanted to assess the entire scene.

He watched as the cop sprinted from tree to tree until he reached the Boss and McKenzie. They were talking, obviously getting ready for whatever was coming next.

AUGUST 24, 9:52 PM

"You're already asleep," Lettie said quietly.

When her two small daughters didn't respond, she stood up from the edge of the bed and went outside. A weak light above the door illuminated a patch of beaten ground. *It'll rain again soon*, she thought as she stroked one of the few remaining tufts of grass with her bare foot.

"Hey!" came from the doorway of the neighboring house. Just as large as hers, and one of a row of eight structures. Window, door, window.

"Hey!" Lettie answered.

Miriam was leaning against the door. "Where are they?"

Lettie had expected Jo-Jo back two hours ago at the latest. The meat and mielie pap had gotten cold a long time ago. Jo-Jo wouldn't care, but she did. She always liked having the whole family at the table.

"Do you think they're at Yonela's again?"

Miriam asked.

Yonela the widow, Lettie thought. A house as large as theirs. As small as theirs. On the neighboring farm. She sold alcohol out of her refrigerator. Illegally. But what else could she do as a widow? She was lucky she had even been allowed to stay on at the farm after her husband's death. The farmer almost exclusively used seasonal workers from around the area, and the houses weren't used much these days. Lettie didn't want to know if Yonela was paying her rent in more than rands.

"They don't have any money with them," Lettie said. "We'd know if they did."

"Yeah."

"But they could borrow some."

"Uh-huh! I wouldn't put that past Sipho!"

"Let's go see Princess."

"Okay."

They walked down three houses. The light over the door was out. All they could see was the flickering from a candle inside. Lettie knocked.

After a few seconds, Asanda stuck her head out the door. She was Princess and Cesar's oldest. She let the two women inside.

Princess was sitting at the table in the middle of the small room. She had her back to the door and didn't bother to turn around when Lettie started to speak.

"Not a trace of them," Lettie said. "What should we do?"

AUGUST 24, 9:59 PM

Gcilitshana reached the two others. "Maybe

they're gone now!"

"We just got one of them!" she said, shaking her head. "I'm surprised they didn't react immediately."

"Maybe we should go back into the house!" Muller.

"Might be more dangerous than staying out here. There's at least fifteen unprotected meters back to the bathroom window." McKenzie.

Gcilitshana studied the path between the fence and house, and agreed that the woman was right. The worst part was that they would not only have to make it back to the house, but they might have to work their way around the building as well if they wanted to reach the front door. Climbing out the window was one thing, getting back through the window was something else completely. Too much time for the bastards to blow them away. "Muller," he said. "I really want to know what you have in the house. Just tell us. They're not just here for a few bills."

"That's ridiculous," the farmer said. "There's nothing here."

"Pssst!" McKenzie hissed.

"What?" Muller said.

"Be quiet! Something's going on!"

A bullet crashed into the tree next to Gcilitshana. Another hit him.

"On the ground!" McKenzie yelled.

AUGUST 24, 10:00 PM

Nobody noticed him as he crossed the hall. Cesar Mhlaba slowly moved one foot in front of the other.

A woman was whimpering quietly. A masculine voice said in Xhosa: "The Boss will take care of it!" Betsie and Jo-Jo. The girls and Trixie were silent. The repairman and the delivery boy were, too.

The door behind which Thabo had just vanished was ajar. He could hear the foreman breathing.

Cesar was convinced from the direction of the sound that the five shots had come from their side. Had to be the Boss or that woman. He didn't trust Gcilitshana in the slightest. He had heard things about him, about how the cop had shot people by the side of the road. You didn't have to believe everything, but you did need to be cautious. Was the cop possibly working with the tsotsis out there?

He was now standing at the door to the room in which Zak had to be located. The door was shut.

Cesar hadn't considered what he might want to do in this situation. He had only envisioned himself with a gun in his hands. That pig standing in front of him, him shooting, done. And now he could really do it. He would do it!

He slowly turned the knob. Well oiled, not a sound. The door opened easily.

Zak was leaning far out of the window. He was holding a heavy gun.

Cesar stepped into the room. He was just taking aim when more shots were fired outside.

AUGUST 24, 10:02 PM

The reception was best up on the rocks. Two bars. Steady.

He had walked back slowly. He had tried twice to complete the call, and then it occurred to him to climb up on the boulders. Even an idiot would assume that the connection would be better from there.

He could see the farmer very clearly from up here. *White skin reflects light*, he thought. As do pale clothes.

The phone rang.

He waited.

"Please leave a message for Dr. Ramesh. He can't take your call right now. Beeep!"

Shit. His inbox.

Alcohol and dagga made a dangerous cocktail. And Ramesh—Dr. Ramesh—always had too much in him. Of both. Sleazy Indian.

He tried one more time: "Please leave a message for Dr. Ramesh. He can't take your call right now. Beeep!"

And again. And again. Then he hurled his phone. Far enough into the field so it wouldn't break.

He stood on the boulder and stomped his foot in frustration. That crap doctor. The phone rang.

Despite the leap from the rock, the landing was soft. He was lucky he didn't hit a stone. He hurried toward the glowing screen, grabbed the phone, and pushed the green button.

"Hey! Doc?"

"Heita, Bro B! Where are you? Doc? Doc who?"

Eddie, the idiot. Why did he have to call now of all times?

"Listen. I'll call you back. Can't talk now!"

"Bulelani, what's going on?"

He hung up. He had to get back.

Shots were coming from the farm again. He started running.

AUGUST 24, 10:02 PM

The policeman was hit. Jayne leaned over and touched him lightly. He grimaced. "My shoulder!"

He was lying on his side, and she patted along his uniform until she felt something damp. He groaned. "That hurts!"

Gunfire was now coming from both sides. Jayne twisted around and fired her automatic in the direction she had just been shooting. She had the impression that the gunfire immediately lightened, although bullets continued to bury themselves into the apple trees and the ground.

"Franz! Shoot in the other direction. Someone's coming that way!"

From where he was lying on his stomach, Franz pulled out his pistol. He flipped onto his left side and fired with his right hand. Slow and controlled. One bullet after the other. And so the two of them fired in both directions.

Jayne emptied her clip and reached for the small pistol in her waistband. She had brought it along for closer distances.

She couldn't see who was shooting at her. Had she missed her target in the bush? Had there been two people there? Had one of them concealed himself nearby? The shooting had stopped from over there. It was also quiet from the other side now.

But now there were shots coming from the

house. She couldn't tell where they were coming from exactly. Or in which direction they were being fired.

Jayne turned onto her back and tried to get an overview of the situation. The cop was injured, though not badly. He still needed to be taken into the house, though. They had covering fire, but their attackers were on two sides, just waiting to kill them.

Or on new orders.

Or on help. Maybe they were hurt.

Or dead?

The shooting stopped for the moment. It had just been a war zone, and now...She counted the seconds. Eight. Nine. Ten. She had to make a decision soon. For the cop.

A burst of gunfire struck the ground beside her. She instinctively pulled herself into a tight ball, and tried to see what was going on with Franz. He started to shoot again.

This attack was coming from the west. She peered toward the north again and fired her pistol at one-second intervals until it was empty. They wouldn't be able to hold out like this much longer.

AUGUST 24, 10:01 PM

More than once, Zak thought he saw something. Or someone. It seemed to him as if there was a pale glimmer somewhere back in the distance. Hidden behind a bush. There where the path led to the neighboring farm.

The shimmer was weak, but steady. And it hadn't moved. Until now.

It was far off, but he watched it draw closer to Dad and the other two where they were standing outside the fence.

Zak tried to concentrate. Used the scope. But all he saw were the old irrigation canals, which offered a good hiding place.

Focus, he told himself. He tracked one of the canals. Very slowly, so he wouldn't miss anything. There was an advantage to knowing your way around. And he knew the farm better than anyone. Except perhaps Dad.

Nothing. He followed the canal back in the other direction.

Still nothing.

Zak lowered his gun and gazed at Dad and the others. They were now lying on the ground. Had someone been hit?

His eyes wandered back and forth between the trees and the canal he had just been following. If the three of them had been fired on from over there, then someone had to be hiding at that spot. From his vantage point, it wasn't easy to survey the entire open area. The small patches of pasture, scattered bits of underbrush, and the uneven terrain offered the attackers numerous options for concealment. Anyone in dark clothing could lie down on such a tuft of grass and be practically invisible.

Now he could make it out more clearly. It was a shirt. Yellow. He just needed to find the figure in his scope. Then...

He reshouldered his gun and studied the landscape again. A gentle draft blew through the room. Strange. He'd closed the door. There was a tiny, dried-up bush. And he recalled seeing the movement somewhere very close to it. He kept looking, in concentrated circles, as he had learned from Dad.

Behind him, he heard the click of a gun being cocked. Right behind him. He jumped up and let his gun tumble down the face of the house. At that very moment, shots crashed through the window and slammed into his chest. Three in all.

One of the three bullets hit his heart.

AUGUST 24, 8:29 PM

"Yeah?" she said into the phone.

The superintendent had forbidden her from answering the phone like this. But first of all, he wasn't in the office this evening. And secondly, you couldn't please everyone all the time.

"Yes, yes," she then said. "This is the police station on Maluti Road in King. And I'm Constable Ncita!" She added: "How can I help you?" She knew perfectly well that the irony wouldn't make its way down the phone line. A white woman on the other end. Concerned, but under control.

"And what are we supposed to do?" she asked in response.

"Drive out?—To the farm?—But it's already dark!—He's probably fallen asleep. Don't worry. —Then he's out checking the fence."

She had almost said that he was probably fucking the maid. Just the day before, Joyce Ncita had read an article that claimed that farmers these days were still having sex with their domestic and agricultural workers. Just like they'd done during Apartheid. Disgusting. Or the daughter of the maid. It depended on the situation.

"All alone on the farm? Alright.—Give me your phone number. It's not showing up on my phone."

AUGUST 24, 10:00 PM

Princess turned to face her visitors. "I'm so pissed off!"

The candle behind Princess flickered in the wind that gusted through the open door. Lettie could hardly see her face. She wondered about the two other women. About why they were so upset. She felt worried, not angry.

"If I have to drag him back from that slut's place one more time," Princess said, "he'll get no sex for a month."

Lettie had heard Princess utter this threat with some frequency. But she also knew it was an idle threat. She liked to put up a front when the women were on their own.

"Should we go over there?" Miriam asked.

"Not without Noluthando," Lettie said.

"I don't understand how she can sleep so hard when Thabo isn't home," Princess said.

"I'll knock on her door." Lettie turned around and walked over to the house next door.

However, before she could knock, the door opened. "I heard you," Noluthando said in her deep voice. "I'm coming!"

AUGUST 24, 10:13 PM

Thabo aimed and fired at the man creeping up

on the apple trees. However, he missed. He had shot often enough, but never at people. And his hand was now trembling despite the fact he knew that shooting the guy was the right thing to do.

He leaned a little farther out the window, trying his best not to lose his balance. The gunfire stopped abruptly.

There was one. For real. In a very garish shirt. He was fiddling around with his gun. Reloading. Thabo trained his sight on him, keeping his shoulders and arms very still. Or at least trying to. And then he fired at the man.

After he shot, he had to search quite a while until he located him again. He was lying on the ground and didn't seem to be moving.

Good.

AUGUST 24, 10:21 PM

She heard crying inside the house. That wasn't one of the girls.

Jayne considered the possibilities. Betsie? More likely Trixie. Was she mourning Rosie? She was certainly entitled to that. But Jayne still wondered.

It had been a few minutes since the shooting had stopped. Or was she confusing minutes with seconds?

Where were the shooters? Had Franz taken out the one to the west? And she the one to the north?

"We have to get Gcilitshana inside." Franz.

"Uh-huh." She stretched and laid her hand on the cop's face. His forehead was hot. "Is it safe?"

"What choice do we have?"

"Come on," she said. "Let's try to pull him through the fence."

She crouched down and tugged on the policeman's feet. He was heavier than she'd assumed. Franz crawled over to the other side to grab him by the shoulders.

"No! Help me over here!" Jayne said. "We can't carry him like that. His injury!"

Franz crawled toward her, and together they dragged the cop through the fence. Jayne then stretched out flat on the ground. She gestured for Franz to do the same.

"Do you think someone is aiming at us?" the farmer asked.

"I don't know. Franz, what's actually going on here? Do you even have a theory about this?"

"No idea."

"Zak?"

"What would he have to do with this?"

"But there's got to be something in the house."

"No, nothing!" Franz turned his head away.

"Now!" a voice shouted. "Come now!"

Jayne glanced up at the windows in the second floor. An arm was waving out of one of them. The foreman. He was waving energetically.

Franz was already getting to his feet. They each picked up one of the cop's legs and hauled him toward the house.

"Keep going, keep going!" Thabo yelled.

A blast of gunfire struck the wall beside Jayne. Thabo responded with a constant barrage against whoever or whatever was out there. Rack, tack, tack, tack. Rack, tack, tack, tack. A second gun came to his aid. Duppuppupp, duppuppuppupp, duppuppuppupp. They pulled the policeman along the wall of the house. The ground was soft. His head would just have to muddle through the best it could.

The cop groaned. "That hurts!"

When they reached the corner, they paused for only one second. The covering fire would provide them some protection from above. And, dear God, let the door be open.

"Quick!" they heard Betsie's voice. "Hurry up!"

Seconds later, they were inside the house. Betsie locked the door just as more shots were fired. One of them hit the door.

AUGUST 24, 8:33 PM

"That's way out there." Sergeant Andile Twaku removed his reading glasses. "It'll take at least thirty minutes to drive it," he said. "Anything else more critical?"

Ncita shook her head. "A missing person's report."

"A child?"

Ncita shook her head again. She gazed at a piece of paper. "Kobus Prins. Seed sales rep. He had several appointments around the region this afternoon. They had fixed supper for him at his B&B in East London. He had ordered it especially, wanted to head back right after..." Ncita glanced back at her paper. "His appointment at Simonshoek. His company called us. They haven't been able to reach him by phone."

"And?"

"Six farms in one day."

"Was van der West's on the list?"

Ncita shook her head once more.

"Hmm. Then we can pick between investigating the stabbing or the farm. Who'll stay here?"

"Simphiwe. She just went out for fish and chips."

"Farm or stabbing?" Twaku asked.

"Farm," Ncita said.

"Alright. Send an ambulance to the scene of the stabbing. We'll take the new Ford."

AUGUST 24, 10:40 PM

Bulelani dashed across the fields. He no longer cared about his shoes. Clean shoes were a concern for tomorrow, now he was worried about the shots he'd heard. He needed to know who was shooting at whom.

The farm was dark when he reached it. He assumed his old post and listened.

Complete silence.

No, there was something.

A man sobbing. Quietly. Suppressed.

What did it all mean? His people were the only ones who'd been shooting. They had hit their marks and killed someone inside the house. The weeping man. One possibility. Both sides had been shooting. The more likely scenario. His people had hit their targets. Again, the crying man. But had the people in the house also hit someone? One other explanation was possible: the shots had all come from inside the house. Unlikely.

Whatever had happened, Bulelani needed to

get the lay of the land.

AUGUST 24, 9:19 PM

Constable Ncita shifted down to second gear. "How long do we have to drive down this gravel road?" she asked.

"We're almost there!" Sergeant Twaku checked his phone. No reception. Swell.

The farmhouse was dark, but a small light-bulb was burning above the front door. The Ford Ranger's headlights transformed the fenced yard into a stage. A padlocked chain secured the gate in the fence that surrounded the house. A bakkie and a small delivery van were sitting on the other side of the fence.

Twaku stepped out of the truck. Ncita followed him but left the engine running.

"What now?" she asked, pulling her phone out of her pocket and checking the signal. No bars.

"Turn the motor off!" Twaku said. "Maybe we'll hear something."

Ncita climbed back into the truck and turned the key. The engine fell silent, the headlights dimmed.

Twaku had already covered several meters by the time she caught up with him. "False alarm," she said. "The farmer's sleeping off his hangover. He'll wake up any minute, see the light, and shoot at us."

The sergeant nodded. "Yes, that's a real danger. I'll just shout!"

He stopped walking and took a deep breath: "Hello! It's the police! Can you hear us? We're with the police!"

"We could use the loudspeaker."

Twaku shook his head. "If he didn't hear me, then he's either deeply asleep or gone. Maybe he has another car."

"Or he's dead!"

"Yeah. Or dead." They kept walking. "How old is he?"

"No clue. The woman wasn't young."

"People die. Heart attack. Circulatory failure. Stroke."

"Maybe he needs help," Ncita said when they finished circling the fence and were back at the gate.

"Perhaps we should have sent the ambulance over here and driven out to the stabbing."

"Wasted time! Come on..."

They went back to the truck. Ncita had already cranked the engine by the time Twaku opened his door.

"Wait!" he said. "Switch it off again."

"What?" she said as she turned the key back off again.

"I heard something. A shot. Or two."

"Inside the house?"

"No. Some distance away!"

"It doesn't have to mean anything. Let's go."

Twaku hesitated. "Okay. Let's go."

AUGUST 24, 10:46 PM

The girls were asleep. Total silence in the house. The Boss and Trixie were holding each other as they sat on the stairs, at the center point between

the ground floor and the second story. The two
girls were sitting above them. Each of them
stretched out on a wide tread. The delivery boy
was draped across several steps, at the same
level as the Mullers. Thabo now knew that his
name was Phumezo. The boy was doing relatively
well. Of course, he needed medical attention, but
he wasn't on the verge of dying. The repair guy,
Pule, sat below him. He hadn't made a sound all
evening.

The situation with the cop looked quite different. He had been hit in the shoulder, and his
injury was serious. He was sitting against the
hallway wall beneath the staircase, and looked
more dead than alive. He would definitely need a
doctor soon.

Cesar and Jo-Jo were sitting on the top step.
Jo-Jo looked resigned to the situation, his knees
drawn up and his head propped against them.
And Cesar...Thabo had caught sight of his worker
running back and forth on the second floor, and
had had to grab and hold him tightly. Cesar could
hardly speak. He was now crouched down beside the hopeless Jo-Jo, staring a hole into the
darkness.

Zak was now lying beside Sipho in the bathroom. On the floor. Less than a meter from his
mother. The Boss had broken down when Trixie
told him about what had happened. Including the
seed rep, they had already killed four of them.
Thabo no longer believed the robbery theory.
Something else must be going on. Must be. He
thought about the story from...years ago. The Boss

and he were out on nighttime patrol. Cattle kept getting stolen. "We'll take care of the problem ourselves!" the Boss had said. Then, they'd come across those two boys. Still kids. The Boss had fired his gun instantly. Thabo had buried the boys in some out-of-the-way spot on the farm. He knew that had been wrong. The families knew nothing about the fates of their children, and should have been able to have their bodies for their own burials. But the worst came weeks later. During a routine check, Thabo discovered that the bodies were missing from their graves. All that remained was loose dirt. He had investigated the graves with a branch he picked up somewhere. But there wasn't anything there. Someone had taken them.

Thabo believed that everything you did in life came with a price.

"Will any of us be missed out there?" McKenzie now asked. She was standing down in the hall-way, gazing up the stairs. But nobody answered. "I mean...Some of us are expected at home. Or somewhere else. Will anyone get worried?"

She waited and then pointed at Pule. "You. Is someone expecting you at home?"

Thabo thought he could see the boy nod. "My mother maybe."

"And what will she do if she thinks you're missing?"

"Call me."

"But there's no reception here."

"She might eventually call the police."

"That would be perfect!" Jayne said. "Why aren't they here yet?"

AUGUST 24, 9:26 PM

"Phumezo what?" Nkosazana Magwaca asked. The white man leaning against the counter couldn't pronounce the name. "Okay. Stolen, you say?"

"Gone!" the white man said. "Probably stolen. But perhaps...anything's possible."

Constable Magwaca pulled a form out of a drawer and jotted down the white man's name from his ID card. "Who does the van belong to?"

"To me!"

"But it's also a Quick Trans vehicle?"

"I'm a subcontractor. I have to have the vans painted like that."

"And when was the car stolen?"

"I don't know if it was stolen. It's gone. The driver hasn't checked in."

"So he stole it," Magwaca said.

"What if he's been attacked? Hijacked?"

"Hmmm. Could be. What do you want to report? If there's no car theft..."

"I don't care. Whatever, as long as you search for my van!"

Constable Magwaca nodded. "When was the last time you spoke with your delivery guy?"

"This afternoon."

"And where was he heading?"

"Here. I brought the list with me."

Constable Magwaca took the list. A few addresses in King and two in Bhisho, as well as several farms.

AUGUST 24, 10:37 PM

"Not so fast!" Noluthando called. "I'm already

a grandmother."

As the four women crossed the old ditch beside the gravel road, Lettie held out her hand to Noluthando. Princess and Miriam were a short distance in front of them.

"Something's not right here," Lettie said quietly to Noluthando.

"Something. And I wish I knew what it was."

"Do you really think they're at Yonela's?"

"I never thought they were."

"What did Thabo say this morning?"

"Somebody was supposed to come and fix the fence. He thought it might take some time, but not this long. It's already dark. Nobody can fix fences in the dark."

Noluthando spoke slowly, emphasizing every word. Lettie understood she wasn't alone in her concern.

"Did you bring the revolver along?"

"Uh-huh!" Lettie could clearly feel it through her shirt, which she had knotted around her waist.

They could hear distant music as they slowly approached the small settlement located on the neighboring farm.

Lettie saw a couple of chairs sitting in front of one of the houses. An older Kwaito album was playing loudly. Only three of the chairs were occupied. Besides Yonela, she recognized two workers from another farm. No trace of their men. She glanced at Noluthando, who was shaking her head. Princess and Miriam were walking back toward them.

"What do we do now?" Miriam asked.

"We'll go to the farmhouse!" Lettie said.

AUGUST 24, 10:42 PM

Bulelani knew that he was fairly well screened by the bush. But if he wanted to see what was going on on the eastern side of the house, he would have to get out into the open. It was definitely dark. But Kaiser's death was proof that he needed to be damned careful out here. The people inside might even have night vision gear. He had seen something about that once on TV. A Hollywood film.

In any case, he would wait to take a look at Kaiser's body until after he had talked to the others. Too depressing.

The window out of which Kaiser had been killed looked abandoned. He had no choice anyway.

It was perhaps fifty meters to the corner of the fence. Then another twenty to the gate and an additional twenty to the Quick Trans delivery van, where he thought Sandi and Enoch were hiding. Bulelani took off at a run.

Yet, even before he reached the bend in the fence, it occurred to him that he'd made a mistake. What if Sandi and Enoch thought he was somebody else? One of the folks from the house, for example. They would open fire.

But he couldn't go back.

No shots from the house. Either the light was too poor for shooting or they were conferring with each other.

Dust billowed up as he rounded the curve. He hadn't made any noise before now. Bulelani struggled to keep his balance. He managed to stay upright, but he stepped on his right foot twice in rapid succession. The two figures behind the hedge were tense, that much he could see. What a pointless situation this all was! He was the ringleader, and he shouldn't be the one running around. He should be giving orders and waiting for them to be carried out.

"It's me!" he called quietly.

"Sure, Chief!" came back.

Bulelani dashed behind the vehicle, ducked down, and leaned back against the driver's door. He was breathing heavily, but was glad he had selected good people.

"What's going on?" Enoch asked.

Bulelani wheezed one more time. "You tell me!"

"They fired over there." Sandi pointed at the north wall.

"And?"

"We don't know why," Enoch said.

"Why didn't you shoot back?"

"You told us to hold our position!" Sandi.

"And we did shoot. Once they all got back inside." Enoch pointed at the farmhouse door.

They weren't all that clever after all, Bulelani thought. He had said they should hold their position, sure. But he had assumed they would keep the situation under control.

"Yeah," Bulelani said. "But everything's changed. Do you really have no idea what happened?"

"No." Enoch.

"There were people." Sandi.

"From the house?"

"Could be." Sandi.

"But who just went in the house?

"The farmer and a woman. And the cop. They pulled him in, though. He's hurt." Enoch.

"And when did they come out of the house?"

No answer.

"Didn't they come out over here?"

"Absolutely not, Chief," Enoch said.

"And when they went in...did you fire?"

"Didn't hit anything!" Sandi.

Bulelani decided that he was more urgently needed on the north side than here. "Wait here." He considered briefly. "If I whistle—I mean, loudly —that means we're attacking. Got it?"

"Yes, chief!"

"Okay."

Bulelani glanced over at the delivery van. Small windows in the house, all the downstairs ones shot out. The same upstairs, but one of them was open. He could see that much. Nobody was standing there and about to fire at him.

It wasn't far to the next fence corner. However, the bushes on the edge of the field weren't so close. And that was where he needed to go. That was where Mandisi and Lulama were standing. Right, Mandisi was the name of Kaiser's cousin. Bulelani glanced around one more time before giving the thumbs-up sign. Enoch and Sandi responded with the same. He took off.

Even before he reached the corner, he knew he wasn't at risk from anyone inside the house. Whatever might be going on in there right now, they weren't shooting. He remembered the man's voice, his weeping. They had hit them. And now they were discussing things.

Bulelani was on his way to the bushes and had already covered most of the distance. He ran the last few meters and crouched down, panting, behind one of the bushes. He hadn't run in a long time. Why would he? Children ran. And athletes. And people trying to get away from the cops.

As he stood up, his jeans got hooked on the bush's thorns. Bulelani cursed. Where were Lulama and Mandisi?

Everything was quiet inside the house. He couldn't hear a single sound. Not even the wind. His mother—who had grown up somewhere near Queenstown—had always said there was no such thing as total silence. There was always something like an animal that you could hear. Bulelani heard nothing. Absolutely nothing.

They could go in now, together. There were still six of them, as long as no one had deserted. And then they'd see who the winners were. But they might get shot to pieces if they did that. Not good. If only he'd gotten hold of Ramesh. That crap doctor!

"Hey!" The quiet word came from somewhere close by.

Bulelani gave a start although he knew the voice, which had a conspiratorial edge to it. He turned around and recognized Lulama's broad silhouette as it tramped toward him across the field. He was breathless although he couldn't have come all that far.

"Chief," he said, as he draped his arm across Bulelani's shoulders. "They just popped up out here. And they shot at us."

"Where is Mandisi?"

Lulama gestured at some spot behind him.

"Dead?" Bulelani asked. "Is he dead?"

"In the head."

"Shit. Where did they get him?"

"Here." Lulama hesitated. "Right where you're standing!"

Bulelani jumped to the side. "Why didn't you say that before?" He gave the other man a shake. "And where is he now?"

"I dragged him over there," Lulama said. "Far enough to the back."

"Why?"

"So that nothing else could happen to him."

"Uh-huh," Bulelani said. "Well done."

Lulama was an idiot. A strong idiot, but still an idiot. He glanced over at the house. There had to be some way to bring everything here to a quick end. "Tell me what happened!"

"They were out here!"

"The people from the house?"

"Yeah. And they opened fire."

"How many?"

"Three, I think."

"What kinds of guns?"

"I don't know. But..." Lulama paused for a few seconds.

"But what?"

"There was a woman with them."

"A police officer?"

"Not in uniform. But the cop who was outside at the beginning was with them, too."

"But what happened?"

"They just appeared out here. And then they shot at us."

"But how did they get out?"

"Through the fence, I think."

"And how did they know where you were?"

"Don't know!"

"What did Sandi and Enoch do?"

"They shot at the house? Maybe. I'm not sure."

"And Mzoli?"

Lulama was silent.

"What is Mzoli doing?"

"I think they got him, too."

"Did you see it happen?"

"I think so!"

"Tell me again what happened!"

"They were outside." Lulama pointed at the grove of trees that was fairly close to the corner of the fenced yard. "And then they fired." A short pause. "We shot back."

"And? Did you hit anyone?"

"The cop."

"Is he dead?"

"They dragged him inside."

"And Mzoli?"

"He came from over there."

"And he also fired?"

"Of course."

"But they got him?"

"Yeah. At some point, he stopped shooting."

This wasn't getting anywhere. Bulelani was

going to have to see for himself what had happened to Mzoli. If he was really dead, that only left four of them, and they would need a completely different strategy. He pulled his pistol out of his waistband.

"If I whistle loudly, everyone should fire. Got that?"

"Uh-huh," Lulama said. But Bulelani didn't think that sounded all that convincing.

He aimed at a window on the second floor and fired three times. Bam. Bam. Bam. Then he dashed off.

It was over fifty meters to the trees, and he hoped his shots would at least momentarily distract them. He couldn't assume that the shooting from the house was over for good. Particularly considering what had occurred when he had tried to call to that crap doctor.

By the time he hid behind a tree, his heart was pounding as if it might explode. He had to hold on to the trunk.

He could hear voices from the house, though he couldn't understand what they were saying or distinguish between the individual voices. But Bulelani was certain that they were scared. A woman now grew a little louder. He looked around.

How many times had he told Mzoli that there were situations in which he should leave his yellow designer shirts at home. They wouldn't need to discuss that problem anymore. His body practically glowed. And the body was lying about twenty meters away from where he was standing.

Mzoli was no longer moving.

Shit, Bulelani thought. First Kaiser, then Mandisi, and now Mzoli. They really were down to four now.

AUGUST 24, 10:58 PM

"Will anyone miss you?" Jayne asked as she dabbed Gcilitshana's entry wound with iodine.

The police officer groaned in pain. He was stretched out on the hallway floor next to the staircase. Jayne turned him over onto his stomach and cut his shirt away from his shoulder.

Franz and Trixie were in the bathroom, where they were sitting beside Zak's body and mourning. Trixie was silent, but Franz occasionally broke down, his sobs deep and long.

As she cleansed the exit wound, Gcilitshana exhaled heavily. "Early tomorrow," he said. "At the office."

"When would that be?"

"Around eight!"

"My maid also comes at eight." Jayne secured the bandage with several adhesive strips. She pulled Gcilitshana's shirt back over his shoulders but left the buttons undone.

"We might all be dead by eight!"

"She will try to call me, but of course, we don't have a signal out here. She won't go to the police. What will your colleagues do?"

The cop pushed himself upright with his back against the stairway wall. "If we're all dead, it won't matter!"

"And if we're not?"

"I don't know."

"But someone in this house has to be missed somewhere. The repair guy said his mother would eventually call the police."

Gcilitshana nodded. "And the other boy? The delivery guy?"

"And what about the farm workers? And Thabo?"

Gcilitshana nodded again. But what could they expect from the workers' wives?

They heard three shots outside. Neither Jayne nor Gcilitshana reacted.

AUGUST 24, 11:04 PM

Vuyo was lying beside the road, holding his injured leg, when the three shots were fired. Far enough away to not pose a danger to him. But that was also what he'd thought when he'd decided to watch the shootout.

But then one of the bullets from the house had hit him, and since then, he'd only been able to move around on all fours. He'd been unable to walk more than two or three steps, and then he'd had to take the weight off his right leg. And crawl.

The wound was in his upper thigh. He was lucky that the bullet hadn't hit him in the crotch. And he was also lucky that the bullet hadn't broken any bones. Nonetheless, he couldn't walk upright.

Vuyo had crawled slowly to the road after being struck by the bullet. And then, meter by meter, down the side of the road toward home. When he heard the voices, he stretched out flat in the dirt.

He was now sorry about the fence. It had been a stupid idea. He knew that Muller always kept cash in his bakkie. In the glove compartment. And he so desperately needed money. He hadn't been able to pay the rent on his shack for the past three months. One more month and he'd be kicked out. He had thought he could cut through the fence, quickly pick the car lock, and get back out of there. But he hadn't calculated on the dogs. He had snipped through only a couple of wires with the cutters when they came at him. Initially to just see what was going on, but then they started to growl. Vuyo was scared, so he ran off before they began barking. He reached his shack in Ginsberg frozen solid and not even one rand richer.

And at this point, he had no idea what was going on here. There were people outside, as well as in the house. The ones outside were shooting at the people indoors and vice versa. That was all he understood at the moment. He was worried about his mother, of course. If he weren't injured, he could run to the police and bring help. And if his phone hadn't been stolen the week before, he could have also called them. He didn't understand that either. The cell signal out here was sometimes bad, but there was still the landline. Why weren't they calling the police?

AUGUST 24, 11:04 PM

Trixie wrapped her arms around her father. She brushed the tears from his face and straightened his sparse hair. She then attempted to help him to his feet, but the old man wanted to remain kneeling beside Zak's body. Here in the bath-room. Next to the others. Next to Mama's body.

He really is an old man, Trixie thought. Now. After today.

When the attack started, Franz Muller had been the man in charge. He was the last person to flee into the house, and then he had immediately started to make the house safer for everyone inside.

Now he was broken.

No, shattered.

Trixie knew that the man she was holding in her arms and whom she loved so much would never again have the strength that had made him who he was in the past.

She hugged her father and began to sob uncontrollably.

AUGUST 24, 11:05 PM

Naturally, it was dark at the upper end of the staircase. Thabo could still see, though, that the two little girls were paralyzed with fear. They were lying in Betsie's powerful arms and were quiet be-cause there was nothing to be said.

Zak had been a stupid boy, but a stupid boy who could fire a gun, Thabo thought. Now they were left with very few who knew how to handle the guns that were in the house. The girls had seen them carry Zak's body through the house.

Muller was now out of commission. The cop was hurt. They had exactly four people to cover the four sides of the house. Mrs. McKenzie, Cesar, Jo-Jo, and himself.

AUGUST 24, 10:12 PM

The telephone rang. Constable Simphiwe Ndwandwa at the Maluti Road Station in King William's Town picked up the receiver and raised it to her ear with deliberate slowness.

"...didn't come home. He never does that. He's a good boy," the voice finished saying before continuing without a pause. "Mr. Bellson can't explain what's happened. He dropped him off, and then he was supposed to take a taxi home. That's what he usually does, but now he's not here. He always lets me know if anything changes. Always..."

Constable Ndwandwa held the receiver out from her ear and let her mind wander. "Let people talk," her trainer at the police academy had said. Give them time to formulate their requests. But he had also said that they shouldn't beat people in their jail cells. Not if there were other possible ways to discipline them. Not everything she had learned was actually a reality when it came to the job. Constable Ndwandwa had already realized that in the two and a half months she had been working here at the station. She pulled the receiver back to her ear.

"Hello?" the voice now said.

"Hello," Ndwandwa said. "What is your name?"

The woman was Mrs. Majola. She didn't give her first name. Her son Pule hadn't come home.

"What should I do? He always calls if he's running late. I cooked supper for him. Mr. Bellson also says that he is very reliable and has never stolen anything."

"Who is Mr. Bellson?"

"His boss!"

"What kind of business does Mr. Bellson run?"

"Fences."

"Fences."

"Yes, fences."

"Like barbed wire and electric ones?"

"Yes."

"To stop intruders?"

"Yes."

"Where...," Constable Ndwandwa had to consider briefly. "Where was Pule's last job?"

"On a farm."

"Yes, but where?"

"I don't know."

"Yes, but what am I supposed to do then?"

"Boss Bellson knows."

"Why didn't he call this in, then?"

"He said that I knew more about how to talk to black police officers, so it would be better if I called."

Constable Ndwandwa exhaled sharply through her nose. "Tell that Boss that he needs to call us himself. Alright?"

As she set down the receiver, Ncita and Twaku walked through the door.

"Did anything happen?" Twaku asked.

Constable Ndwandwa shook her head.

AUGUST 24, 11:08 PM

He would have fired.

He absolutely would have done it.

Cesar Mhlaba was sitting with his back against

an upstairs wall, trembling all over. The gun was sitting across his legs. He was supposed to have long been back at his post, but he couldn't hold his gun still at the moment.

He had been only one second away from shooting the pig in the back. His finger had been on the trigger when the shots flew in from outside. He had thrown himself on the floor as the Boss's son was hit. And then the bastard had just lain there, and he had quickly slipped out of the room. What could he have done anyway?

"Cesar? Hey, Cesar!" Jo-Jo was standing in front of him. "Come on. We're supposed to go down. Discussion time."

AUGUST 24, 11:12 PM

His shoulder hurt terribly. At least it would keep him from having to go back out with that crazy woman. She was now organizing another meeting. The workers had come downstairs for that. And the repair guy. Gcilitshana froze while he listened to Jayne McKenzie speak.

"We need to man the windows again soon. They are still out there," she was just saying.

No one replied.

After a hesitation, Jayne continued. "If we leave Franz and Trixie to themselves for now, then there aren't so many of us left."

"We still have enough to cover the windows." Thabo.

"Not if we go back out." Jayne.

"Is that necessary?" Thabo.

"That's dangerous." The repairman.

"Does anyone have a better idea?" Jayne.

Silence.

Trixie stepped out of the bathroom and joined the group. "We're all going to die." She then went up the stairs.

More silence.

"There are still three or four people out there," Jayne said after a while. "And as long as it's dark, they have the advantage. We have to take that away from them."

Further silence.

"I need someone to go with me!"

It was suddenly dead quiet. Gcilitshana could hear Muller who was still in the bathroom. The farmer was sniffling. A woman was speaking tonelessly upstairs. Trixie. A bird chirped.

"I'll come," someone said. It was the foreman.

AUGUST 24, 11:12 PM

Bulelani stared at the farmhouse. He was furious. Not because Mzoli was lying dead at his feet. Or because of Mandisi or Kaiser. But because everything had been planned differently. Everything could have gone so smoothly.

He had to talk with that crap doctor. But there was still no reception. Bulelani stomped westward. Hopefully, he wouldn't have to go so far again to pick up a signal.

AUGUST 24, 11:19 PM

"Muller!"

The farmer had just come out of the bathroom. He sat down without saying a word. Gcilitshana placed his uninjured arm across his shoulders.

"I know," he said, "this is a bad time. But it's also just a shitty night. None of us could have seen this coming, right?"

Muller didn't respond.

"I know you've been hit hard, Muller. But something...There must be some explanation! For what is happening here."

Muller shrugged his shoulders a little.

"No idea?"

Head shake.

"Have you really told us everything?"

Muller took a deep breath and slowly released it. "Listen: I've had no idea what this was about from the beginning. As far as I'm concerned, the people out there can take whatever they can find in here. At least, at this point."

"But what would they find here?"

"Forty or fifty thousand rands. The guns. A little jewelry, heirloom pieces."

Gcilitshana knew that this was ample motivation for a farm attack. But he also knew that the counterattack against the assailants had been strong enough for them to have beaten a hasty retreat. Which hadn't occurred.

"Anything else?" he asked. "Drugs?"

"Huh?" Muller now turned to look at him. "Nonsense!"

"Your son. Or maybe someone else?"

Muller thought fleetingly of Vuyo and about the fact he had disappeared. But Vuyo was a scrawny beggar. He couldn't even afford a pair of new shoes. He wasn't mixed up with drugs.

AUGUST 24, 11:14 PM

He was cold. The slight daytime warmth from the winter sun had vanished long ago. And he couldn't get off the ground.

Vuyo was moving slowly down the side of the road toward the farmhouse. He knew that he was heading into the center of the danger, but his curiosity was greater than his caution. And maybe he could do something for Mama there. He didn't care about Muller. Or the rest of that white family. He couldn't make it home as it was. He was too injured for that.

I should've told her goodbye when I left the house, he thought. He'd just left when the others had been busy with other things. He couldn't take it anymore. Everyone had something to do. Everyone had a program to follow. So obvious, so fixed. He was the only one without a job. And Muller didn't want to give him one.

There weren't any jobs anywhere else, either. He had no money at all. It was so frustrating. Which was why he'd wanted to go home that afternoon. The distance to Ginsberg was long. And he couldn't afford a taxi. So he'd slipped away early. But he should have said goodbye.

Mama was probably really worried about him. Or maybe not. Perhaps she was glad he was gone. Got out ahead of time. Though probably not as early as she might have thought. He had heard the first shots and had run back. He had wondered about the van parked by the side of the road. Did it have something to do with the attack?

The filth from the road and the fields had

worked its way up his sleeves. His thin shoes were damp. His neck ached because he'd had to hold his head up for hours.

Had it really been hours? Vuyo had lost all sense of time. There was the fence up ahead.

Where could he go from here? They were shooting from the house. At the people who were hiding somewhere out here. Maybe even close to him.

"The Chief's plan doesn't seem to be working," someone nearby said. "Does it?" the same voice said a few moments later. Deep. Mature.

"Hmm. I don't know." A different voice.

Not even ten meters away. Vuyo hardly dared to breathe.

"He really should've told us more." The second voice was a higher-pitched man's voice. A little melodic. "It's okay to bring us in on a job, and then to do it and divide the take. Even if he gets more than us. But here..."

"At least one of us is dead. He has to tell us more."

"What do you know?"

"That everything was supposed to go really fast. We were going to kill a few folks and get away quickly."

"But with what?"

"Don't know."

"Have you seen anything today that could've been what we were supposed to get?"

"Hmm. Not really."

"But what could it be?"

"Money?"

"But why here?"

The two men stopped talking. Maybe there was nothing else to say. Or they needed to consider the possibilities.

Vuyo had never seen piles of money around the farm. But nobody would have shown him that anyway. On the other hand, the cop was here, the one he'd never seen. And the fat man he didn't know either. He listened hard into the night, but the two men had finished their conversation.

AUGUST 24, 11:28 PM

"There's only two of us now," Thabo said. Jayne and he were sitting in the prayer room, gazing out the window.

"There are four of them. I think. We shot two of them when we were outside. And I killed one of them beforehand. Out the bathroom window. Can you run with your leg?"

"It'll be fine. I'm no longer a spring chicken, Madam."

Jayne laughed. "It's been a few years since I was a schoolgirl, too. And please...don't call me Madam. I'm Jayne."

"Hmm. Okay, Jayne." Thabo tried. It didn't feel right. And under other circumstances, she wouldn't have invited this familiarity. "How do we want to do this? Do you have a plan?"

"The others know about the hole in the fence now. Either we look for another way out, or..."

"If there's covering fire, it might work. They'll be kept busy, and we could try the same place again."

"Yes," Jayne said. "Perhaps." She didn't sound

convinced. "Above all, we have to depend on each other," she said. "Do you trust me?"

Thabo was startled by the question. The Boss had never asked him this.

"Uh-huh," he replied.

He didn't trust himself to ask her the same thing.

AUGUST 24, 11:28 PM

Noluthando went first. Her years on the farm outnumbered the lifetimes of the other women. Lettie was at her heels, revolver in hand. A few years ago, Jo-Jo had taught her to shoot. He had at least shown her how to hold the thing. The other women cheered up when Noluthando brought up the episode again. At the time, they had all laughed over it.

Now Lettie was following Noluthando. In the darkness, she had no idea where they actually were. Princess was behind her, and Miriam brought up the rear.

"Watch out," Noluthando said. "Thorns."

That had to be the blackberry vines on the neighboring farm. They still had a ways to go until they reached Boss Muller's farmhouse.

Since leaving Yonela's place, none of them had said very much. An occasional warning about an obstacle along their path, or a comment about how or where the track was going. That was it.

At the same time, none of them were frightened in the dark. They were used to the darkness, considering how often their electricity went out. And the paths from the county road to home were always long. They all knew the dangers of the darkness. That wasn't it.

Something didn't feel right. They agreed on this, without even discussing it. Each of them knew it. And each of them knew that there was more going on than just a missed supper.

"It's slippery here," Noluthando said. "Watch out!"

AUGUST 24, 10:38 PM

Sergeant Andile Twaku wiped his hands on the paper napkin. He was thinking about his wife and the promise he had made to her that he wouldn't eat anything greasy after eight o'clock. Because of his weight. But his profession meant that he couldn't always be picky. He couldn't just watch the two women eat. Besides the fish was just too delicious. Having a beer along with the fish and chips would make everything perfect. But he was still on duty.

The telephone rang. The two women weren't in the station lobby. Twaku was surprised that the evening had been so quiet. Hardly anyone had walked in off the street. However, he knew from experience that it didn't pay to praise the night before daybreak.

The phone was still ringing.

"Police. Maluti Road Station. Twaku speaking."

"Bellson. I was supposed to call."

"Okay. Why?"

"Because of my repairman."

Twaku looked around. He was still the only one in the lobby. "Who did you talk to?"

"With my repairman's mother."

"Ah!"

"But she had just spoken with you."

"Just tell me what happened."

The other end of the line was silent for a moment. "Well..." Twaku listened as the caller gathered his thoughts and then began to talk. About a young repairman he had dropped off at a farm. He had more jobs than he had people and vehicles. Everything was urgent. Had to be taken care of immediately. Customer satisfaction. So he had driven the boy out to the farm. When he was done with the job, he was supposed to go to the closest paved road and call for a taxi to take him home. Only he never reached home.

And, Twaku thought, *what does this have to do with me?*

The boy was never late, and this wasn't like him, the other man added. Twaku jotted down a few details, as well as the phone number and name of the caller. And then hung up. He set aside his pen, and tossed his empty fish and chips container into the trash. He turned around and was about to go to the restroom.

Simonshoek? The caller had said Simonshoek. Hadn't there been something else going on out there?

Twaku hit the redial button and called the man back.

AUGUST 24, 11:28 PM

Bulelani stopped walking. He heard voices ahead of him.

He could see a weak light from that direction. He checked his phone. No signal.

Children's voices. A girl. A young woman? Bulelani saw the outlines of houses. He hadn't even thought about the farm workers. The poor pigs. Under the thumb of the whites. No supermarket, no liquor store nearby. And definitely no TV channels.

He caught sight of the girl, who had stuck her head out the door of one of the houses. But if there were houses here, then there also had to be a trail somewhere close by. He wouldn't have to keep plodding through filth and gravel.

The terrain gradually grew hilly. Bulelani strode uphill, making a wide curve around the houses. The higher he went, the better his chances were of finally being able to place a call. That much was clear.

When he reached the ridge, he looked around. He saw the lights of the city in the distance. Was that really King William's Town? Didn't matter.

He saw two out of five bars light up on his phone. Finally.

"Please leave a message for Dr. Ramesh. He can't take your call right now. Beep!"

Shit. He tried again. And again.

The crap doctor wasn't available. He hadn't even turned off his phone. He was just stoned somewhere. Son of a bitch.

AUGUST 24, 11:41 PM

Lettie held the gun stretched away from her like a piece of rotten meat. She could handle it—at least, a little—but she wasn't used to holding it. To be precise, she had only picked something like this up a couple of times, just to practice. Jo-Jo had said that sometimes it was useful to know how to shoot. He sometimes said: "This is a dangerous country."

They couldn't be too far from the farmhouse by now. They had left the fruit trees and berry shrubs of the neighboring farm behind them a while ago.

"Shhh," Noluthando said from right behind her. Lettie stopped.

"I don't want to be in front of you," Noluthando had just said. "You should lead the way with that thing."

When Princess and Miriam caught up to them, Noluthando said: "We don't have far to go now."

"There it is," Princess said. "Behind those trees."

They all looked in that direction.

"Really?" Noluthando.

"Yes." Princess.

"My eyes are no longer all that good. In that case, be quiet."

"But it looks just fine here." Miriam.

"Still!"

Lettie didn't know what to do with the revolver, so she stuck it back under her shirt against her hip. They stood there and listened.

"Should we shout or something?" Princess.

"No!" Noluthando's voice lost its cheerful edge and now sounded sharp. "We'll first take a look around."

The wind shifted and blew lazily in their

direction. However, it didn't carry any sounds to them. Only the scent of an extinguished fire. Maybe from a grill.

"There's something." Miriam.

Lettie didn't hear anything. "What is it?"

"It's...," Miriam said. "It's...I'm not sure, but it sounds like someone's crying. But it isn't a woman. It's a man."

"Cesar has never cried." Princess. "Not even when..."

"Shut up!" Noluthando.

Lettie tried to hear the crying man, but the wind grew louder. And then a nearby cricket started to chirp.

"Look." Miriam. "There's something on the ground over there."

The other three women looked about and tried to catch sight of what Miriam had seen.

"It's yellow!" Princess moved toward it. The others followed.

Princess suddenly inhaled sharply and stopped in her tracks. "He's dead!"

All four of them knelt down around the man's body. No one said a word. Lettie instinctively pulled the revolver out from under her shirt. This body had a dark, bloody hole in its chest. And it wasn't cold yet.

"Okay," Noluthando said as she slowly got back on her feet. "This isn't what I imagined was going on here. We should get away from the yellow spot. Immediately."

AUGUST 24, 11:38 PM

Trixie tried to sing quietly. The girls needed to sleep. The shooting had stopped for the time being.

But her voice simply didn't want to work.

It was dark in the guestroom, but she could still sense that the girls were watching her.

"Where's Grandma?" Britney asked.

"Grandma's sleeping," Trixie said. "She'll join us in a little while."

AUGUST 24, 11:42 PM

Jo-Jo was feeling sick. The Boss's son had just been shot in the very spot where he was now standing. And he couldn't remember why he was here.

Ah, that's right. To save his life. His own life. As well as Cesar's and Thabo's. Okay, and maybe Betsie's, too.

He balanced the gun on the windowsill and knelt down onto the floor. Now he was fairly well protected. He didn't want to die saving the Boss. The Boss wouldn't save him, either.

On the other hand, it would be good if the Boss didn't die. He paid them, after all. Ideally, everything would be over soon.

There was a spot farther back in the darkness. He had to squint in order to see that far. But he knew what he saw. It glowed like a plastic bag out in the pasture. And it was yellow.

And something was moving around it. He could see better now. Maybe he could do something to help this night come to a quicker end.

Jo-Jo had never used a gun with a scope on it. He pressed his right eye against the back end of the metal tube. And searched. It took him a few moments to locate the group. There were three shadows. No, four. And they were kneeling around the yellow spot.

AUGUST 24, 11:36 PM

"I got one of them." Thabo pointed out the window in Zak's room. "He was definitely dead. Someone must have moved the body."

Jayne and he stared outside for several minutes without saying anything. For the first time, he sensed that this woman was afraid.

"Mmhm," she now said. "There was another one. We got him back there. Looked like a clown. But there," she pointed in another direction, eastward, "there should be others over there. If they haven't redistributed themselves by now. But..." She leaned out the window and gazed to the east. "I wish I knew how they were positioned."

Thabo didn't say that he was the one who had shot the guy in the yellow shirt.

Jayne began to pace back and forth. "If we can take out the leader, then the group will come apart. How do you think they're organized?"

Thabo had never attacked a farm. Or a bank or a supermarket. But he knew one thing clearly: "Someone came up with the idea and hired the others. That is the Boss behind it all. But what if he's already dead? Maybe we took him out of the picture."

Jayne sat down on the bed. Thabo thought

about Zak who had spent last night there asleep. "In any case, they haven't shot for quite some time," he said.

"It's possible," Jayne said. "Yes. But I don't think so."

"Why not?"

"There was a break before the last round of shots. It was a fairly long one at that. If we had managed to kill the leader during our first excursion out there, then they would have split before then."

"And what should we do now?

"I would like to go out the other side this time. Out the living room side."

"But there aren't any trees over there for protection."

"We'll go out there anyway," Jayne said. "It might even be a safer spot for us."

AUGUST 24, 10:49 PM

He hadn't really listened to the man, but he had called back, at least.

Now Sergeant Andile Twaku had a second missing person's report that had something to do with this farm. Simonshoek. He spread a local map out in front of him. It showed King William's Town and its townships, small Bhisho—the capital of the Eastern Cape—and other locales like Zwelitsha and Breidbach, as well as the entire region with its numerous villages and farms.

Simonshoek was a large farm. He had even been there once, as Twaku recalled. But why had that been?

The two women returned at the same moment the outside door opened. A thin, old man peered inside. He then pushed the door open wider and approached the counter.

Twaku reached for the phone book as Ndwandwa greeted the old man.

He dialed the number he found. The phone at the farm was dead.

He pulled his cell phone out of his pants pocket and pressed several buttons.

"Eita!" Constable Magwaca said on the other end of the line.

"Listen!" Twaku said. "Have you heard anything about Simonshoek?"

"Why do you ask?"

"We have two missing persons tied to the farm."

"Two? Wow. We've also gotten one."

"Who?"

"Wait, I'll check. That piece of paper is somewhere...just a second...Here it is. Phumezo Mrwetyana. A Quick Trans delivery guy."

Twaku steadied himself against the wall. "He's not one of ours."

AUGUST 24, 11:48 PM

Jo-Jo was still concentrating on the four figures who were standing around the yellow spot on the ground. Hadn't Mrs. McKenzie said that there were probably still four people outside who were waiting until everyone inside was dead so they could take whatever it was they were looking for?

Maybe he could end it all.

Jo-Jo tried to stay totally calm as he gazed through the scope. Four figures, that was correct. But something out there didn't feel right. If what he saw wasn't an optical illusion, at least two of the four figures were wearing skirts. They were women. And the other two were as well. One of the others had a silhouette that reminded him of Lettie.

He instantly took his finger off the trigger.

AUGUST 24, 11:33 PM

Bulelani went back up the hill. He had been part way back to the farmhouse when an idea came to him. However, first, he tried to reach the doctor one more time.

"Please leave a message for Dr. Ramesh. He can't take your call right now. Beeep!"

He then tried a different number.

"Yes?"

"Pastor, hey. It's Bulelani."

"My friend! What's going on?"

"I have a problem. Could you use a little extra money?"

"I'd be lying if I said I didn't."

"Listen! We're out in the country, not too far out. A quick snatch and grab job. So we thought."

"Keep talking."

"Diamonds. Delivered yesterday, to be picked up some time tonight. A helicopter's going to take them to Maputo."

"If we don't step in?"

"Exactly."

"Who's behind it?"

"I don't have all the details. But an old farmer is supposedly handling it. His son deals in diamonds, and someone in the local government will get them out of the country quickly."

"If we don't step in!"

"Yeah."

"So, why hasn't it worked out the way you'd planned it?"

"Beats me. There were more people out here than I'd thought there'd be."

"And where do I come in?"

"If you can get out here, we can storm the farm. We'll take what we want and disappear. You shouldn't come out here on your own, though."

"How many do you have?"

"Four."

"How many did you start out with?"

"Seven."

"What if four of us come?"

"Perfect, man."

Bulelani explained to Pastor how to reach the farmhouse.

AUGUST 24, 11:41 PM

Cesar hoped he wouldn't have to shoot. And that everything would be over soon. But he hadn't been able to refuse. There were too few of them at this point, which was why he was now standing in the prayer room and staring through the scope.

He gazed into the darkness. The moon had slipped behind the clouds a few minutes ago. He could still make out the shapes of things.

He saw a wide landscape composed of gray tones. The trees and bushes along the road. And a crocodile very close to the road.

Cesar concentrated. That didn't make sense. Front leg, back leg, front leg...then drag. And again. Front leg, back leg, front leg, drag. That wasn't a crocodile. It was a person.

The colors were what didn't fit the rest of the scene. It was hard to distinguish them, but he could now see the white or light color on its feet, a red or green—he wasn't sure—on its upper body. Gray underneath. He moved his finger onto the trigger.

The crocodile moved in short, little jerks. One shot, and it wouldn't move ever again. If he hit it. He hadn't used a gun more than three or four times. But the thought was exhilarating. And now he could liberate the crocodile from its life. He felt his cock stiffen.

AUGUST 24, 11:03 PM

"The fact that the phone is out doesn't mean anything. This happens all the time to the one I have at home."

Sergeant Twaku couldn't stand Inspector Robbie van Vuuren, but he was right about this.

Van Vuuren was the highest ranking officer on duty tonight in King William's Town. And on this conference call, he had the final say. Van Vuuren was black, but not really. There had to be some white blood in his family tree. His skin was too pale. And there was his name. A Boer name. They regularly cracked jokes about him.

"What should we do then?" Twaku asked. "Yet tonight."

"Drive out there!" van Vuuren said.

The constables Magwaca—on van Vuuren's side—and Ncita—on his side—were also involved in the conference call. Nobody said anything for a few seconds.

Ncita interrupted the silence. "Are you going out or are we?"

"We should both send out a squad car," van Vuuren said.

"Why, Chief?" Magwaca asked.

"Just a hunch."

"What kind of hunch?" Twaku asked.

"Hmm...The kind of hunch that tells me that something out there isn't right."

"And how should we do that? With safeties off?" Twaku asked.

"Safeties off!" van Vuuren said.

AUGUST 24, 11:54 PM

He followed the road.

More like a track. But a car might drive along here anyway. Careful. He had twisted his left ankle slightly two different times among all the many holes.

Bulelani felt certain that the farmhouse couldn't be too far from here. But he couldn't know that for sure. He was always out of his element whenever he left the city. How were you supposed to keep your bearings out here?

He needed to move away from the road soon. He didn't know what had happened while he was gone. He needed to first assess the situation and then get it back under control. And then wait on Pastor and his people. Take care of everything quickly. He didn't plan to leave anyone alive. No kids, either. There couldn't be all that many security guys in the house.

Maybe he'd spare the children.

A dull sound in the distance. Far, far away. But strange enough to make him stop and listen.

Bulelani instinctively took two steps away from the road and hid behind an old tree.

He instantly recognized the sound for what it was. But it took Bulelani a second and then another second and then yet another second to formulate the word *helicopter* in his mind.

The sound slowly grew into noise, and he wondered where the loud chopper would land. He arched his neck upward and watched as the dimly lit helicopter flew over his head and over the farmhouse. Or at least over the area where he assumed the farmhouse was located.

Bulelani gazed after the lights in the sky. The chopper suddenly dropped its speed and hovered in the air for a moment. And then it landed on the other side of the horizon.

Beyond the horizon was also beyond the farmhouse. Far away from it.

South Africa was a free country. And helicopters could land wherever they wanted. He didn't know how many of those machines were actually in the Eastern Cape. But he did know one thing: It was unlikely that there were two helicopters landing on the same night out in the country near King

William's Town.

Something had gone wrong.

AUGUST 24, 11:53 PM

Betsie, Trixie and the girls were back in the prayer room. Cesar was still staring outside.

"Everything will be fine," Thabo said, more to the women and girls than to Cesar, as he shut the door.

He had seen that in a film once. The hero had said something like that before going out. To hunt bad guys. Mel Gibson. Or Bruce Willis. And that was exactly what they were about to do, too. Hunt the villains. He felt quite sick whenever he thought about opening the door and...what specifically? Waiting on the people outside to finish him off.

Mrs. McKenzie was waiting for him in the doorway to Zak's room. It would always be Zak's room to him, even now that he was dead.

"It's alright," the delivery boy said, who was sitting on the floor and leaning against the wall of the room. "I'm not feeling all that bad." Thabo had already forgotten his name.

The other boy was standing at the window. The one who was here because of the fence. He was holding the pistol as if it were a spoon. There was no way he had ever fired one before. Jayne stood behind him for a moment, straightened his back, and helped him to point the gun. That was all she could do.

A helicopter flew over the farm. The noise ebbed rapidly away.

Jo-Jo joined them. "Outside, there are more..."

"More?" McKenzie.

"Lettie." Jo-Jo.

"Who's Lettie?" McKenzie.

"Where's Lettie?" Thabo asked. "She must be at home."

"She's out there," Jo-Jo said. "And she's not alone."

AUGUST 24, 11:53 PM

"We have to go back," Noluthando spoke very quietly. "I don't know what just happened, but out here, they can see us from the house. And I don't know if everything is okay in there. Come on."

Lettie followed Princess and Miriam to a small boulder behind which Noluthando had already ducked.

"Who was that?" Princess asked.

"Who do you mean?" Miriam.

"The yellow man!"

"Be quiet!" Noluthando.

All four women were now kneeling behind the boulder that was only half as tall as they were. To Lettie, the farmhouse looked like a large, dark shadow. The apple trees in front of it, to the left. A row of bushes stood to the left of them. And way in the foreground, the yellow shirt that glowed so brightly in the darkness.

"Okay," Noluthando said. "A dead man is lying there. He's been shot. Close to the farmhouse but not inside the fence. What could that mean?"

Lettie recalled a story her sister had once told her. She was living on a farm close to Queenstown. A friend of her sister's lost her job when the farmer and his wife had been shot and killed in an attack. People had come during the night, had shot the two of them in the head, and cleaned out the house. It had been right before the next payday, but the workers hadn't seen another rand.

Something reminded her of that now. But things were different here. And the yellow man had nothing to do with the farm. Besides, they had already been paid for the month.

A dull noise came from somewhere, quickly growing louder. None of the women said anything. They gazed into the sky and watched the helicopter pass. *If this were a movie*, Lettie thought, *it would land here and save everyone. All the good guys, that is.*

"An attack," Princess said as the noise slackened. *Yeah,* Lettie thought, *what other answer could there be?*

"But what happened?" Noluthando.

No one said anything. It was completely silent.

"And where are our husbands?"

Again, nobody said anything. Before this point, Lettie hadn't imagined Jo-Jo being in danger. But the man in the yellow shirt...wasn't from the farm. She suddenly felt stone cold. But why were their men missing? And if they were inside the house, why was it so dark?

"Watch out!" Princess ducked even lower behind the boulder.

"What is wrong?" Noluthando.

"There's someone over there!" Princess spoke so quietly that the others could hardly hear her.

A tall figure was moving between the trees.

From one trunk to the next. He was using the cover the trees provided to remain hidden from the windows. He then took off at a run and knelt down beside the yellow shirt.

AUGUST 24, 11:41 PM

Pastor looked around the shebeen. He saw a few people he'd worked with before. Relatively reliable, but too drunk. With Crazy, he had robbed a couple of old women who had just collected their pension payments. That had been a fairly good hit, but when one of the women had snuffed it during the attack, they had abandoned their plans. Crazy hadn't really needed to bloody that woman's head. Now he was having a hard time holding his beer bottle. Willis, who was standing beside Crazy, was always good if guns were being fired. But he was currently staring down the cleavage of the girl standing across from him. He had other interests at this moment. You had to respect that.

Pastor walked back outside, sat down in his new Golf, and started to make phone calls.

AUGUST 24, 11:39 PM

Sergeant Andile Twaku brought the Ford to a screeching halt in front of the Alexandra Road Station. Constable Ncita wasn't wearing her seat belt. Catching herself against the dashboard, she stared at him reproachfully.

"Well?" Inspector van Vuuren asked. He was already standing in the station entrance, Constable Magwaca beside him.

"Well?" Twaku said. "It's probably nothing. Power outage at the farm. The seed rep is ordering expensive wine somewhere. The delivery guy is fucking some girl. And the other one...he's doing something else."

"Yeah, I bet," van Vuuren said. "But it's still a little much. Three missing persons."

"That's why we're driving out there," Twaku said. "But how do we want to proceed?"

"Let's cut off our headlights before we reach the farm," Constable Magwaca said.

"Hmm," van Vuuren said.

"But we're the police," Twaku said. There was no reason to hide, in his opinion. "There's no reason to hide," he added.

"Headlights on?" Ncita.

"Headlights on." Van Vuuren.

"So...we'll drive up, have our guns out, and then what?" Ncita.

"We'll look around." van Vuuren said.

"Emergency lights, too?" Ncita asked.

"That would probably make sense." Van Vuuren.

Two minutes later, Twaku and Ncita were sitting in their Ford once more. Van Vuuren and Magwaca followed them in their older Nissan. Both vehicles drove with their emergency lights on.

AUGUST 24, 11:59 PM

"You have to, Franz!" Jayne was kneeling beside the farmer on the stairs.

She took his head in her hands, and it occurred to her that she never would have done this if

Rosie were still alive. Such an intimate gesture.

"You have to. Who else could do it?"

Muller didn't move.

"Come on, Franz," Jayne said as she took his hand and pulled him off the stair. Thabo stood a little to the side, staring in the other direction.

Jayne dragged Muller upstairs and into the second-floor bathroom. Muller's best gun was already sitting there underneath the window.

"We're about to go out, Franz. And you have to cover us. Got that?"

Muller nodded.

That was more than Jayne had expected. "You'll see us in just a minute. From here. And it will be up to you if we survive this."

Jayne then explained to Franz what he needed to do.

AUGUST 25, 12:02 AM

Lettie extended her gun arm and aimed. She wasn't sure if she could hit the man, but he definitely wouldn't be coming any closer to them.

She felt a hand on her arm and turned to gaze into Noluthando's face. Despite the darkness, she could see the tension in the older woman's face. She shook her head.

"What do we do after you fire?" Noluthando whispered into her ear.

The man straightened up, but instead of retracing his steps, he crouched behind the bush where the yellow man was lying.

The bush couldn't have been more than twenty-five meters from the small boulder the women were hiding behind.

AUGUST 25, 12:08 AM

Bulelani watched the dark silhouette of the farmhouse and didn't move. He had no desire to trip over Mzoli's corpse. But that was exactly what would happen if he went back the way he had come. And Kaiser's body was stretched out on the other side of the house. Just as dead. Just as unpleasant to see.

He didn't feel bad that Kaiser was dead. Or Mzoli. But they both reminded him of how much had already gone wrong out here.

Bulelani decided to make a recon run along the front section of the farmhouse. And to find Kaiser.

AUGUST 25, 12:06 AM

There wasn't much left of the large window-pane. A few jagged pieces stuck out from the frame, which had also been practically obliterated. Lying on their stomachs among glass shards and wooden splinters, Jayne and Thabo peered outside. Jayne pointed at the shot-up police BMW. "We need to get to the area between the car and the fence." What she didn't say was that the man she believed to be the ringleader was standing somewhere on the other side of the fence.

Jayne and Thabo fell silent for a few moments.

"I think," Jayne then said, "that it'll be safer on the other side of the car than on this side. At least some of them won't be able to see us over there."

They crawled along the bottom of the window

and stood up. Thabo opened the wooden door to the terrace. Quietly. He slowly pulled it open, remaining concealed behind the door. With her gun cocked, Jayne knelt on the floor and aimed at the opening. When nothing moved outside, the two of them dropped back to the floor and cautiously made their way out of the house. They left the door open.

AUGUST 25, 12:11 AM

He could smell Kaiser before he saw him.

That wasn't normal. Normal was for there to be victims on both sides in every confrontation. Like during the attack on the armored car two years ago. Or was that three? Two of the guards had died immediately. But the third had been tough and had refused to stop shooting. Bulelani eventually managed to escape, but he was the only one. Just barely. And without any loot.

He never saw the bodies of the others again. They had been picked up later by the police. Their pictures had been in the newspaper. That was completely normal. The fact that he was now kneeling next to Kaiser's corpse wasn't.

Bulelani touched the body. He snatched his hand back briefly when he felt something damp. That had to be blood. He continued searching, reached into Kaiser's pants pocket. It was also damp in there, but it wasn't blood. He drew out a wallet and stuck it into his own pocket. He then turned Kaiser over and pulled the pistol out of his waistband. He found an extra clip in his jacket.

AUGUST 25, 12:11 AM

Her faith must be strong, Thabo thought as he crawled behind Mrs. McKenzie. And she was much quicker than he was. She was definitely fit. At some point, he had overheard a conversation between the Boss and his wife about how much she worked out. And she had two healthy legs. In his case, every other movement along the ground was slower and shorter.

McKenzie was already sitting with her back against the BMW when he reached the vehicle. She was holding the gun, ready to fire at any moment. Thabo sat himself up beside her.

He was afraid. And he was thinking about Noluthando. What were the women doing right now? There was no time to give them any thought. It had to be close to midnight. *There are only four of us left*, he thought.

Actually only three. *Poor Sipho*, Thabo thought. Poor Miriam. Alone with the children.

Seriously. What would his wife do if he didn't come home? It wasn't really all that late. Things like this never happened to him. Almost never, anyway. Would Noluthando come over to the farmhouse? And the others?

Hopefully not.

Thabo glanced up at the house. He could see a black, metallic tube in the bathroom window. The Boss was standing behind it. Mrs. McKenzie had said that they would wait on him.

AUGUST 25, 12:10 AM

Miriam stood watch and peered over the top of

the boulder. The other three women had sat down on the ground and were talking as quietly as they could.

"So, it's nighttime," Lettie said, switching the gun to her other hand. "He doesn't belong here. He's trying not to attract attention to himself. And he has something to do with that body. We have to do something. Whatever he's up to isn't good for us."

"But what?" Noluthando asked. "Anything we do will make noise. We could try to capture him. If we do that, there will be a lot of yelling. Or he's armed and there will be even more noise. And we don't know what's going on inside the house."

"He's not waiting around to ask the Boss if there are any odd jobs here," Princess said. "I think we should shoot him."

"And then?" Noluthando.

"Then...we'll see." Princess.

"And our husbands?" Noluthando.

"In the house!" Princess.

"And if not?" Noluthando.

"Where else could they be?" Princess.

"Wait a second!" Lettie said. "If our husbands are inside the house, then that's strange. They're never inside."

"Thabo is sometimes inside with the Boss," Noluthando said. "But the others normally aren't. The longer we talk, the more I like the idea of shooting him."

"But," Lettie asked, "what if I miss him?"

AUGUST 25, 12:10 AM

"Pull yourself together!" Franz Muller told himself as Jayne and Thabo crept over to the bullet-ridden car.

Over the past hour, he had tried to think about God, but the connection never materialized. He had then considered killing himself, but then God came to mind again and he remembered that suicide was an unchristian thing to do. He had very briefly considered simply going out with two guns blazing and killing them all. He wasn't worried about what would happen to him. But then Jayne had given him a task. Perhaps that was the best thing that could have happened to him.

Thabo reached the car. Muller saw that his supervisor had trouble turning over on the ground, because of his lame leg. But Thabo was a tough nut. Tough on himself and on others. Muller recalled an incident that he hadn't thought about in a long time. They had been coming out of a hardware store in East London, and Thabo had nabbed a boy that someone had said was a thief. He had first stuck out his leg so the boy tripped over it. Then Thabo had thrown him up against the bakkie and beaten him with the new broom they had just purchased until blood ran from the boy's head. Eventually he had kicked the boy in the back of his knee with his stiff leg and told him to get out of there.

What had Jayne said? Once we reach the car, give us a few minutes. If nobody shoots at us, we'll stay there quietly for a little while before continuing. Jayne was now back on her knees and peering around the edge of the police car.

Muller took a deep breath and did what Jayne had instructed him to. He aimed his gun so that he fired over the fence, one shot after the other.

"Ching, ching, ching," Jayne had said. "One a second. And move the gun from right to left then back right. That would be the best way to do it."

AUGUST 25, 12:14 AM

"Follow me!" Jayne said to Thabo. She crawled around the car on all fours, her gun clutched in her right hand.

She couldn't see anything beyond the fence. Darkness, several shadows, bushes, a few trees that had been left standing. She hesitated, tense. Muller would start firing any second now. What was keeping him? Had it been a mistake to involve him again after the deaths?

Ching, ching, ching, ching. There it was, finally —the high-pitched sound of the automatic gun. Jayne leaped to her feet and sprinted the short distance to the fence. As she ran, she pulled the small clippers out of her pocket and started working on the fence as soon as she reached it. Thabo joined her shortly after that. As agreed on, he took her gun out of her hand.

Ching, ching, ching. Muller was firing at a steady rhythm. Jayne tried to match it and to cut the wire at the same intervals. That worked until the first bullets came flying from the other direction. Deeper, unrhythmically. Somebody was responding to the gunfire.

She tried not to let this disturb her. As long as

Muller kept going, the other man couldn't aim. Couldn't be sure. That was the plan.

And then the other bullets stopped. He had been hit. Ching, ching, ching. Muller was shooting like clockwork.

But then there was the sound of completely different shots. From farther away.

AUGUST 25, 12:16 AM

As the first shots fell, Bulelani was sitting on his heels. He had tested the weight of Kaiser's pistol in his hands, and it had felt good. He had already stuck the extra clip into his jacket.

He was enough of a professional to throw himself immediately onto the ground. He heard one bullet strike close by. In something hard. A branch perhaps. From where he was lying on the ground, he cocked Kaiser's pistol and pointed it toward the house. And fired.

Until it was empty.

AUGUST 25, 12:17 AM

Muller did nothing more than what Jayne had asked of him. But he felt himself growing relaxed. He had always enjoyed shooting. And this wasn't all that bad. Covering the entire area with bullets without knowing what they were doing to whatever they were hitting calmed him down some.

Muller didn't hear the other bullets.

AUGUST 25, 12:18 AM

Jayne tried to push the bullets out of her thoughts, the ones that were being fired by a third party somewhere. Maybe one of the workers had caught sight of a tsotsi.

She cut as quickly as possible. Her right hand —the one holding the clippers—was slowly growing stiff. She knelt down to cut through the wire on the lower half of the fence. Shots were no longer coming from the other side. And now the ones from the third gun had fallen silent.

She had almost reached the point that the hole was large enough. They had to be able to fit through it, but she didn't trust it yet. Nor did she trust Muller completely. Before they passed through the fence, he would need to stop firing.

"On the ground!" she said to Thabo.

AUGUST 25, 12:19 AM

Bulelani curled himself into a tight ball after emptying his gun. He wanted to get away as fast as possible. Other shots were being fired somewhere else. He covered his head with his arms and waited.

But only for a few seconds. Then he was completely calm. Was it over? Reload? *Whatever*, he thought.

He jumped up and ran in a straight line away from the fence.

AUGUST 25, 12:15 AM

Lettie, Noluthando, Miriam, and Princess were still sitting all together, but they hadn't said anything in a while.

The present situation was clear. The man over there was an enemy.

As the ching-ching began, Noluthando shook Lettie's shoulder. "Now!"

Lettie was trembling as she stood up from the cold ground. She leaned her pelvis against the boulder and raised the heavy revolver. The gunfire that had just started continued undiminished. There—where the man had just disappeared beside the bush—he now came back into sight. Lured out by the shooting. Lettie could clearly see his back, because he had turned to face the house. She stretched her arms one more time and fired. And then again. And then again.

Until the gun was empty.

AUGUST 25, 12:15 AM

When Franz Muller started firing his automatic, Betsie was sitting in the prayer room. She put her hands over her head. She knew the bullets couldn't reach this spot, but she still felt the need to protect herself. She was also thinking about Vuyo. Whatever the boy was up to, at least he wasn't on the farm.

Cesar was kneeling down at the window, several meters away from her, and gazing through his scope. He had just had the crocodile in view and was only one second away from firing, but then the gunfire distracted him and he lost his target. He searched all around for it. He wanted to fire, too.

Trixie was stretched halfway across her daughters, hoping the girls wouldn't wake up. She had been scared for a while now that the worker with the gun—she had forgotten his name—would start to fire. The children would definitely wake up if that happened.

Vuyo was chilled to the bone by the time he heard the first shots. And although his adrenaline surged, he didn't feel any warmer. He rolled away from the edge of the road into a ditch and stayed perfectly still.

Alfred Gcilitshana was still sitting below the staircase. He had started to feel a little better. He was slightly feverish, but the pain in his shoulder hadn't grown worse. When Jayne McKenzie and Thabo crawled outside, he experienced a second of euphoria, knowing he didn't have to go with them. But that feeling ended with the first shot. He wondered if he was really safe where he was sitting.

Something happened around the yellow spot when the shooting started. Jo-Jo could still see the figure, and he could have fired. The only problem was that he was no longer certain that he had the right target in front of him, not since he had recognized Lettie's silhouette outside. Had he just dreamed that? He stared fixedly at the figure. The gunfire continued. Shots started to come from some other direction. And now close by, too. Jo-Jo kept his gun trained on the figure. It twitched, then again and again. It crumpled to the ground. Simply pitched forward. But he hadn't fired.

Who had?

AUGUST 25, 12:23 AM

Bulelani ran.

He kept running even after the gunfire stopped.

He then stumbled over something and fell.

He ran his hands down his clothes and found dirt, but nothing was torn. He cursed anyway. Nothing was going right today, absolutely nothing. He stood up and brushed the dirt off his jacket and pants.

Taking a deep breath, he listened to the night. No sounds, nothing. How eerie. There were always noises in the city. Something to help you get your bearings. Something that told you if danger was nearby. Or wasn't. None of that applied out here. Here you could die without any warning whatsoever.

On some shitty farm! Imagine that. Things usually turned out very differently. The city always beat out the country.

The next steps were quite clear. Back to the house, inform the other three about the finale to this affair, wait on Pastor, have a quick confab, attack, kill all survivors, collect the jewelry, money and guns, and then vanish into the night.

It was almost twelve thirty. By this point, he would have ideally knocked back a couple of whiskeys already. Maybe had sex with one of the girls from the shebeen where he liked to celebrate. Instead, he was rolling around in the dirt like some animal. He put his phone up in his pocket.

And pulled it right back out again. Instinct. Four out of five bars. Almost the best reception possible. He still had one phone call to make.

AUGUST 25, 12:24 AM
Crawling through the hole in the fence like a

kid had made his leg start hurting. Mrs. McKenzie was lying very quietly on the other side. Thabo did the same.

It was a noisy night. He hadn't noticed that before now. No time for such things. But as the last shots died away, he realized how deafening the chirping was. A hadeda was screaming down from a tree. Something on small paws was on the move nearby. Probably the farm cat. She was lucky to still be alive. Car noise, but Thabo had no sense of how far away it was. Or from which direction it might be coming. Voices from the house? Where else could they be coming from? He couldn't make out any words.

The helicopter had just flown over them, and he had fleetingly wondered if it was a police rescue chopper. Not because of him. Nobody would crank up a helicopter for him. And not because of Jo-Jo or Cesar. Nor because of Sipho, who had been dead for quite a while as it was. But maybe because of the Boss. And his family. But then the helicopter kept flying.

Thabo crawled one more meter to join Mrs. McKenzie. "What do we do now?"

"I don't know!" she said.

AUGUST 25, 12:16 AM

Lettie was still standing in the same spot, both arms outstretched and shaking.

Noluthando gently pulled her down to the ground. "There's a lot of shooting going on. We have to be careful!"

"Do you think I hit him?"

"More than once."

"Did you see it?"

"Of course, I did!"

"What do we do now?"

Nobody made a sound.

"Maybe it's all over." Princess.

"And then?" Noluthando.

"We'll look for our husbands. Inside the farm-house." Princess.

"If they're there." Miriam.

"And if it isn't all over?" Lettie asked. "That was —what do they call it?—a real shootout. Like in a war. And either somebody's won now, or it'll start up again in a little bit. And even if someone has won, it might be the wrong side, right?"

"So let's wait." Noluthando.

"Maybe!"

"I think so, too!"

AUGUST 25, 12:17 AM

The county road was empty. The two police cars were making good time, their emergency lights still flashing. It had been a few minutes since they'd had any interaction with van Vuuren and Magwaca in the second vehicle driving behind them.

"What do you think has happened?" Constable Ncita asked. She glanced over at Sergeant Twaku who was leaning over the steering wheel.

"The flashing lights don't make driving any easier," he said.

"Just turn them off."

"But we all agreed to keep them on."

The two of them fell silent for a few minutes.

"I don't know," Twaku continued. He gazed into the rearview mirror and noticed that their colleagues had fallen back a short distance. He dropped his speed. "Maybe a power outage."

"I don't think so."

"I don't think so, either."

"Then why'd you say that?"

Twaku needed thirty seconds to come up with an answer. "To keep my hopes up."

"What do you mean?"

He needed even longer for this answer. "This is South Africa," he said. "It isn't unlikely that we'll find the farmer and his wife and the three missing men all dead. Their guts hanging out. Heads chopped off. Knives sticking out of their groins."

"Are you serious?"

Twaku was serious, but he also enjoyed shocking Constable Ncita. She was still wet behind the ears, and it was worth the effort, as he had just confirmed.

Sergeant Twaku had another reason for saying these things. It was always advisable to expect the worst. If you expressed the horror, and then found the parents in high spirits and the children fast asleep instead of with bullet holes in their temples and stab wounds in their stomachs, then that made everything all the better.

"Shit," Ncita said.

"What?"

"I forgot the spare ammo."

"At the station?"

"Pull over for a second!"

Twaku cut on his blinker and gradually dropped his speed.

"What's going on?" came across the radio.

"Just a minute," Twaku said.

He brought the car to a stop on the side of the road. The second vehicle stopped behind them. Ncita got out and searched her floorboard. She then crouched down and reached under her seat.

"There it is," she said, pulling out the clip.

The bakkie that passed her was doing almost 200 km/h. The two police vehicles vibrated in the backdraft. Ncita looked over at Twaku, who shrugged. "Want to go after them?" he asked into the radio.

"We have more important things to do," they heard van Vuuren reply.

AUGUST 25, 12:17 AM

"But we have to do something. Now!" Princess stood up and rubbed her eyes. "What are we waiting on?"

"And what should we do out here?" Noluthando asked. She sat down with her back against the small boulder and crossed her arms.

When no one responded, Noluthando continued. "Besides, we're out of bullets now."

"No, we aren't," Lettie said. She held up her hand and shook it. The cartridges rattled clearly in the small cardboard box. "We have some more." She paused. "Maybe twenty or so."

"If you end up using them the way you did the last ones, those will only be enough for three more tsotsis," Noluthando said.

"Do you think they're tsotsis?" Miriam.

"I saw one of them," Noluthando said. "I didn't recognize him. And there was no reason for him to be out here. Not at night! The other man had something to do with him. Who else could they be? Other than tsotsis, I mean."

"And you think there are more of them?"

"What we just heard was a shootout, not a hunt. So...yes!"

"What should we do?" Miriam.

Lettie wasn't sure if she actually meant what she was about to say. "We should go up to the house and see what's happened."

"How do we get there?" Noluthando.

Lettie pointed at the apple trees. "Along there!"

"Do we all have to go?" Miriam asked.

"Do you want to stay here by yourself?" Noluthando asked in return.

AUGUST 25, 12:24 AM

The three men sitting in the old bakkie weren't his ideal business partners. But sometimes beggars couldn't be choosers. Pastor knew all three of them, at least. A few years ago, he had made a little money with one of them. The other was a frequent drinking buddy. And he knew that the other guy earned a living from burglary. For the amount of time he'd had, this was a fairly respectable result. And one of them had brought along a car with a powerful engine. That meant he didn't have to take his new Golf down the dirt road.

The occupants of the two police vehicles

pulled over by the side of the road were obviously searching for an address. Good thing they were otherwise occupied. His car was faster than theirs, but having the cops on their heels would have put a serious damper on their activities.

He needed to pay attention now as he tried to follow Bulelani's instructions. Pastor hit the brakes and kept his eyes out for the guide markers. Something that started with "Simon."

There it was. The farm sign: "Simonshoek."

Things would now get interesting. How was the gravel road? And how long would they have to drive?

Pastor cut off his lights and continued through the darkness in second gear.

AUGUST 25, 12:26 AM

"But we have to do something," Thabo said. "That's why we came out here in the first place."

Jayne was glad that Thabo couldn't see her roll her eyes. She had no idea what they should do next. They'd been lucky to survive that last crossfire. Who had shot at them? Had that been the leader of the tsotsis? She recalled the tall figure she had seen behind the bush and tracked through her scope. Good Lord. That had been hours ago. They had been stuck in this situation for hours already.

"Mrs. McKenzie..."

"Jayne. Please call me Jayne."

"Yes...okay. We have to get out of here."

"What do you think we should do?"

"I think that he ran toward the south. Away

from the house. That's where we should go."

"Why do you think he went that way?"

"Because that was where he had the best odds of escaping the Boss's bullets."

"And why should we follow him?"

"Because he won't expect us to."

Jayne tried to understand Thabo's reasoning.

"And because we'll see him before he sees us," Thabo said.

"Because we can wait for him somewhere and he won't be expecting that."

"Exactly! He will have to come back eventually."

"And when we see him, we can take him out?"

"That's it!"

AUGUST 25, 12:30 AM

"Please leave a message for Dr. Ramesh. He can't take your call right now. Beeep!"

Shit shit shit!

Bulelani tried again.

"Yes...Hello?"

It was really him. "Doctor," Bulelani said.

"Who is this?"

Bulelani had to bite his tongue to keep from yelling at the doctor.

"Doctor. It's me. We've been busy this evening. Did you forget?"

"How late is it?" Bulelani heard rustling and the scrape of a chair. The doctor then cleared his throat. "Middle of the night. Where are you?"

"Where do you think?"

"And how did it go? You know I don't like to have these kinds of conversations on the phone."

"Yeah," Bulelani said as he made the snap decision to kill the doctor the next time he saw him. "Yeah. We're still out here. Nothing's happened. There were people at the farm, a lot of them."

"Well, we're talking about a major take," the doctor said. "You don't have the loot yet, do you?" He whistled through his teeth. "You've had enough time already."

Yep, he was going to kill him. "It didn't work. They fired back."

"I told you so."

"And the helicopter flew past the farm."

The doctor fell silent.

"Doctor. Did you hear what I said? The chopper didn't land here."

"I heard you. Yes."

"So..."

"Hmm. I would say that either you're on the wrong farm or the helicopter took a wrong turn."

"What's the name of the fucking farm again?"

"Simonsvlei!"

"That's it!" Bulelani said.

AUGUST 25, 12:30 AM

Twaku slowed down so he could read the sign more easily. "Simonshoek" was written on the sign, and underneath it, "Greetings from Franz and Rosie Muller." He kept the car in second gear as he drove down the dark road, but then shifted to third and accelerated. The first pothole made him slam on the brakes. It was deep, and he almost lost the car in it. He cut his speed back down.

How ridiculous, Twaku thought. *We have all our*

lights on, but we can't even drive 20 km/h.

AUGUST 25, 12:27 AM

Noluthando went first. She gathered up her long skirt and ran across to the apple trees. The other three women watched her. Nothing happened.

Lettie thought that it had to be safe over here. From what they had heard, all the shooting was on the other side of the farmhouse.

"Reload," Noluthando had said before she took off. "And cover us!"

Princess was the next one. Lettie held the revolver gripped in both hands out in front of her. As Princess reached Noluthando, Lettie could feel Miriam's eyes on her.

"I'm so scared!" Miriam said.

"But it's safe."

"Not for myself," Miriam said. "For Sipho." And then she took off at a run.

Lettie waited a few seconds after Miriam reached the others before sprinting across the stretch. She avoided looking at the man she had shot only a few minutes before.

AUGUST 25, 12:30 AM

The police cars' flashing lights were still visible. Pastor wondered why, but he didn't have time to give it much thought. It was hard enough to drive down this track without lights.

"What are we going to do?" one of the three asked. He was sitting right behind the driver's seat and his breath smelled so foul that Pastor almost felt nauseous.

"First of all, we're going to be very, very care-ful," Pastor said. "That's why we turned our lights off. And once we get there, we'll wait on my contact. He asked us for help because his little job hasn't gone as planned."

"You already told us that," the other man in the backseat said. "But what's this all really about? What are we going to steal?"

"Money, I think. A few guns, too. We'll have to take care of the other people out here, but my contact says it'll be worth our time."

"Good call," the foul-breathed one said. "This late at night, it better be worth it."

He deserves to die for that stench alone, Pastor thought. If there really were diamonds out here, then there was another reason. Why should he have to share?

AUGUST 25, 12:37 AM

Bulelani weighed his options. He had run this far out because of the gunfire. He had heard that some weapons had a firing range of over a mile. That had to be about as far as he was from the house. Which was why he had no time to lose. He needed to get back there as fast as he could. After all, he was the chief. But he still had to be careful.

What was the worst that could happen now? Pastor could show up at the farmhouse with a few assistants. Unannounced. Enoch and Sandi would open fire immediately. And what would the people inside the house do? They'd shoot, too. It could turn into a total bloodbath. That was what would happen if he didn't get back to the farmhouse in time.

The first thing he needed to do was fill Enoch and Sandi in on the new plan. Lulama also. But that wasn't as critical, because of where he was standing. But it could be catastrophic if Enoch and Sandi didn't know what was going on.

On the other hand, maybe it wouldn't be so bad. If enough people got wiped out on both sides, then it might be easier to finally get his hands on the loot. However, in order for that to happen, enough people had to die inside the house. Considering the lay of the land at the moment, this was the factor that remained unpredictable. Which was why he had to get back. Bulelani decided not to run, but to walk. Caution was always more important than speed. And you never knew who might be lurking behind the next bush.

AUGUST 25, 12:35 AM

Franz Muller felt less troubled after he fired. Since Rosie's death, there hadn't been a single second in which he could gather his thoughts. And then Zak had died, too. For a short time, nothing had mattered even a little. If a bullet hit him, so what? But then he remembered Trixie and the girls. And Pat and his family, regardless of how far away they were. He still had a reason to live.

When Jayne and Thabo crawled through the fence, he stopped firing. Muller thought about his foreman. He had underestimated him all these years.

He now glanced through his scope. This thing was amazing. You could almost see as well as you could during the day. He should have thought to use the gun earlier.

He examined the area beyond the fence. Something was out there.

"Dad," he heard a voice he knew very well. "Dad, do you think we're going to get out of this alive?"

He had been focusing on whatever it was he had discovered when Trixie laid her hand on his shoulder. He lost his target.

"Dad," she said. "Luckily, Britney and Christina are fast asleep. But I don't know what to tell them anymore. Dad...Why are they out there? You have to know something."

Muller pulled his gun out of the window, flipped the safety on, and placed it on the floor. He then wrapped both arms around his daughter. As he offered his child the desired shelter, he thought about how there was no one left to shelter him. To take care of him. Under other circumstances, he would have sent Trixie back to her room as had been agreed to. But he knew that he needed this hug as much as his daughter did. "Dad!"

Trixie freed herself from his embrace.

"Dad! Why is this happening?" she said loudly.

"Shhhh! Not so loud. We don't know who's out there!"

"You really don't?"

"No, sweetheart. I really don't know why all this is happening."

After taking Trixie back to the prayer room,

Muller picked his gun up again.

AUGUST 25, 12:32 AM

This was insane! What were they doing here?

Jo-Jo watched the four figures that were hiding behind the trees. He had already identified Lettie. Now he recognized the others. Princess and Miriam. And even old Noluthando. They had barely been able to defend themselves. And now they would somehow have to get the women inside the house, too.

Jo-Jo left his window and went downstairs. He took his gun with him.

AUGUST 25, 12:38 AM

Jayne crept along the cold ground, wishing that she was wearing more than just her leggings and t-shirt. This was definitely not enough. Black was good, thin not so much. It was winter, after all. Her movements grew awkward as she felt increasingly chilled. Following her, Thabo was panting at the effort. They needed to take a break, if only to give the foreman an opportunity to catch his breath.

An old irrigation ditch appeared in front of her, from the time before they'd installed overhead sprinkling systems. Ditches like this hadn't been used in a long time, and Jayne was surprised that this one still existed. She crawled into it and gestured for Thabo to follow her. She then turned around so their heads were close together.

"Everything okay?" she asked.

"Everything's fine! I'm just not used to this. The

crawling, that is. What should we do now?"

"Maybe wait here?"

"Why here specifically?"

"We're close enough to the house that we can still see it. But we're far enough away not to get shot from there. And..." She glanced around. "And I think that whoever was just shooting will have to pass by close to here. If he hasn't already done that."

Thabo didn't ask any other questions, but she kept talking. "I suspect he wants to get to the gate side. To the east. There are probably other people that way. And one more person to the north. We don't know what he knows, but I think he'll go that way. And we have a good spot here."

"And if he comes by?"

"We'll shoot."

"And the noise? What'll happen when we start to fire?"

"Yes," Jayne said. "We'll have to take that risk. If we can hit him in the head..."

AUGUST 25, 12:39 AM

"What should we do now?" van Vuuren rasped through the radio. "I suggest that we leave our lights on and take a look around. It will probably be just fine out here. Any objections?"

"That would be fine with me," Twaku said.

"But," Constable Ncita asked, "if things aren't alright?"

"What do you mean?" van Vuuren.

"I mean...There are three people missing. That is strange enough, right?"

"So? What are you trying to say? That we're going to stumble across a massacre out here? One in full swing?"

That's not all that impossible, Twaku thought. He had already cracked a few jokes about this. But they had all seen their fair share of massacres before now. The multiple murders, raped babies, and beaten-to-a-pulp grandmothers. This was why he said, "It's possible."

"Okay," van Vuuren croaked. "I'll still ask— what should we do now?"

Twaku hit another pothole and swore. Nobody else said anything.

Constable Magwaca finally spoke up. "I'm afraid," she said quietly.

No one answered this.

"Alright," van Vuuren continued. "This is what we'll do. We'll drive up to the house and wait at first. Let's say...for a minute. If everything looks safe, we'll get out with our guns in hand—okay?— and take a look around. We will stick together as a team, and the gangsters won't even have a chance. How does that sound?"

"Okay," Magwaca said.

"Okay," Ncita said.

"Okay," Twaku said.

"Besides," van Vuuren resumed, "it's the middle of the night. Whatever might have happened on the farm, you know the statistics. Farm murders occur either early in the morning or early in the evening."

AUGUST 25, 12:39 AM

If he hadn't just stepped on a dry twig, he would be moving quietly. Very quietly. Bulelani could make out the outline of the farmhouse, and he stopped. *If you can't see much*, he thought, *you have to listen more carefully.*

He concentrated. Blocked out everything else. There was more going on out here than he'd thought. Here in the country, in the night. Human voices mainly.

It was whispering. Very quiet whispering at that. But that meant that they were very close by. Bulelani also knew whose voices they were. He'd had better things to do than watch them. They had only been a marginal consideration during those seconds when he had been forced to fire. With Kaiser's pistol.

But they had been there. Two figures who must have come from the house.

Must have.

MUST HAVE!

Now they were outside. And Bulelani understood what had occurred during his absence when he had been talking to that crap doctor. When he had run into that other farmer. They had sent out a squad. A hunting squad. To liquidate him. Him and the others. That had happened, and this was still their plan.

Bulelani was amazed at how selectively the brain functioned. He finally understood what had happened at the fence. And even if he hadn't seen everything, he knew one thing for sure. The two figures—or had it been three, no, two—hadn't been security professionals. They would have mowed him down already.

He could still hear their voices, and he slipped over toward the spot where he thought they were coming from. He had to grin.

AUGUST 25, 12:36 AM

"Do you see anything?" Noluthando asked.

They were standing behind the trees, and Lettie wondered why they were actually hiding. Considering that they were trying to stay concealed behind the apple trees, they must think the danger was actually inside the house. But she wasn't so sure. In any case, the yellow guy and the other dead man were outside the house.

"Do you see anything?" Noluthando asked again.

"There are people at the windows!" Princess. "I think they have guns. I can see black tubes."

"But who is it?" Miriam.

"Can't tell." Princess. "I can't see anyone, but they're there. I know that much. Look, there..."

Nobody can see where Princess is pointing, Lettie thought. And she hoped nobody could hear them, either.

"...there. The one tube is now gone."

"And?" Miriam asked.

"It's just gone," Princess said.

"And what should we do now?"

Princess and Miriam fell silent.

"We'll wait," Lettie said. "Something will happen. And then we'll know what to do!"

AUGUST 25, 12:44 AM

Locating the spot again wasn't turning out to be all that easy. Muller stared through the scope, wondering what it was he thought he'd seen. He peered far out into the fields, and lost his ability to concentrate because everything looked the same.

Something had moved along the ground, but he had only caught sight of it for that fraction of a second before Trixie had come in.

Everything looked the same after dark. Various shades of gray, occasionally almost white and sometimes practically black. Fascinating what all this scope could do. In reality, it wasn't anything more than an upgraded telescope. He now saw something again, something very dark. Concealed somehow, distinct from the fields in front of it. A different kind of darkness. But nothing more than a couple of bewildering contours.

One of the old irrigation ditches. Of course. A good hiding place. But for whom? Could Jayne be hiding in there? Along with Thabo? Had the two of them stuck together? He hadn't been able to listen in when they had discussed their plans. He just hadn't been in a condition to focus. He now cursed himself for that.

If he wasn't mistaken, something was moving in the ditch. Not much, just enough for him to notice it. If Jayne and Thabo were waiting there, they were fairly far away from the house. Did they have a reason for that? Was that their plan? Or had they simply not found a better place to hide?

Muller kept searching. Slowly, in tight circles. His father had shown him how to do this. "If it's dark in the morning, this is the best way to find the bok."

Bulelani felt like a thief. All the slinking around, barely daring to breathe. Not his philosophy. Thieves were cowards. People who operated behind others' backs. Furtively. He, on the other hand, was an entrepreneur of strength. If he wanted something, he took it. It was nothing more than a question of power relationships.

The soil in this fucking field was softer than in the others, as if it had just rained. Bulelani placed one foot in front of the other, very carefully. A low sucking sound was being made by the ground, hopefully they hadn't heard it. He was quite close now. The voices had been quiet for a little while, but he knew. He knew where they were hidden.

Bulelani pulled his personal pistol from his waistband, and cocked it as quietly as he could. He took the gun in both hands and pointed it into the darkness in front of him.

"And if he doesn't come?" Thabo was cold, and he had begun to lose faith in Jayne's idea.

She was smart. She was energetic. No doubt about that. But the waiting was wearing him down. And if he needed to fire his gun any time soon, he would have a hard time bending his fingers. Because of the cold.

"Then we'll need a new plan."

"Should we go back to the house?"

"Hmm...We have to attack them where it will hurt the most. They're still standing at the gate. If we can knock out two of the four, they'll be finished."

"And then what should we do?"

Mrs. McKenzie had to think about this before answering. "We should wait until dawn. They won't have any protection once the sun rises. But they'll disappear long before that, anyway."

Thabo finally realized what she was saying. He wasn't sure if they were really strong enough to force the remaining tsotsis to give up. There was a quiet sucking sound nearby. Quite nearby. Thabo wondered what was making that sound. It was dry, but the Boss had told them to water a few spots. *But in that case*, he thought...He heard another sound. It was so low he wondered if he had misheard it. And yet, quiet or not, the cocking of a pistol always had a menacing ring to it.

AUGUST 25, 12:43 AM

Son of a bitch! He'd almost driven off the road.

"Shut up!" Pastor bellowed. "Just let me drive!" He was holding the steering wheel with both hands, his arms outstretched and his back pressed firmly into the driver's seat.

"When we get there, the first thing we'll do is listen to what my contact has to say. Then we'll attack the house."

As he spoke, Pastor was astonished that he could still see the flashing police lights. That had to be some kind of brand new technology.

AUGUST 25, 12:46 AM

Muller kept searching and couldn't help thinking about his father again. Back then, no gang of blacks would've even thought about attacking a farm and randomly murdering people. These days, nobody ever said anything favorable about Apartheid. That could land you in a hot mess. But in terms of security, the Apartheid folks had kept the country under control.

Eventually, the circle he was making with his scope would be too large. Muller started reducing his radius. It was obvious that he needed to stay vigilant. He just knew what he was looking at all too well. After all, everything he saw belonged to him. Literally every tree and every shrub. Even the dead tree over there that looked like a person holding something out in front of him. Everything was his. And he had wanted to leave it all to Zak. Tears welled in Muller's eyes.

"Pull yourself together!" he ordered himself.

And then it occurred to him that a dead tree could never stand there like that. This was his property, and there were no dead trees on it.

Panicked, he began to search again for the object he had just seen but not recognized. He swung his gun back and forth without recognizing anything. He then stopped and took a calming breath. Started over.

He knew precisely where he had caught sight of movement in the irrigation ditch. "This is my farm!" He confirmed this fact by expressing it. And there, there it was. The ditch. And the person. Or the two of them. He registered that someone alive was still in there. Cautious movements. Two people stretched out head to head? Muller continued to search the surrounding area.

The ditch was located between a field and a hedgerow that was no longer being tended. He ran the scope along it, first in one direction, then in the other. He shifted his gaze a little away from the bushes, and there he was. The tree was swaying. A tall man in dark clothes, that much he could see. He was heading toward the hedgerow and the spot behind which someone was lying in the irrigation ditch. The man was holding something in his hand. No, in both hands.

Franz Muller knew exactly what it was. He tried to remain completely calm.

And he aimed.

Then fired.

AUGUST 25, 12:49 AM

Right before Franz Muller fired his shot and missed Bulelani, the four women who were hiding among the apple trees heard the sound of a car. Brakes, opening doors, then the shot. It was Lettie who said: "Okay, the car, we don't know who is sitting inside it. And we also don't know who just fired. If someone inside the house shot at the car, then there is no way it is a police car. But who's in it?"

"We'll just stay here for now," Noluthando said.

At that moment, Princess noticed the two figures who were obviously trying to hide from the new vehicle.

"Hey!" Jo-Jo called, waving.

But the shot had cut him off, and the women hadn't heard him. He was now considering what he could do. He didn't know who was in the car that had just driven up. And the shot changed everything. He pulled himself back inside the bathroom window, climbed over the bodies, and cocked his gun. He then walked over to the terrace door.

Pastor had come to a cautious stop. All four riders opened their doors at the same time, like in a gangster film. And then the shot had been fired. They dropped down onto the dusty road and pulled out their guns. And waited for the next shot.

Bulelani knew he'd been lucky. He had heard the shot and the simultaneous crack of a branch in the hedge. He had instinctively thrown himself on the ground and then immediately jumped back on his feet. Thank God he hadn't dropped his gun. He then took off at a run for the farmhouse.

Several seconds before the shot, Thabo had Mrs. McKenzie on the shoulder to signal that they weren't alone. They both quickly rolled onto their sides, their guns cocked and ready. They waited for something to happen. What they didn't expect was the shot. They winced in unison and ducked their heads. They heard the bullet hiss through the hedge sitting only a few centimeters away from them. And then a quiet squelching sound. Thabo believed that whoever had been standing on the other side of the hedge had been hit. He had hopefully dropped dead. Jayne wasn't able to classify the noise as quickly as Thabo. It reminded her of the sound of a refrigerator door being opened, but she knew that there weren't any refrigerators out here in the fields. When the other person started panting, they both knew that someone was running away on the other side of the hedge.

The shot hadn't been all that bad, but Franz Muller didn't exactly know that. He was having trouble finding the spot in the hedge again. When he took the shot, the gun jumped a little in his hands. He was now searching for the spot again, so he was a little late in noticing that something was happening at the gate. He hadn't heard the car pull up. Someone began to call in Xhosa, and although he understood and spoke the language, nothing except the raw tones themselves made it through to him. He leaned out the window, but it wasn't easy for him to see the car that had just arrived. Several people were beside it, but the angle wasn't good enough for him to fire. Besides, he had no idea whose side the newcomers were on. Franz Muller saw a strange light in the distance. Almost like heat lightning, but ascending and descending. He couldn't make rhyme or reason of it.

Cesar had tried to relocate the crocodile, but he stopped when he caught sight of the light on the horizon. Were the police actually on their way out here? Who could have called them? What might have happened? As the car pulled up, he watched as two figures abandoned their safe spot behind a bush. Cesar pulled up his gun and took aim. But then the car parked, and he hesitated.

All four doors opened at the same moment, and at practically the same second, a shot was fired. All four men who had just stepped outside fell to the ground. The one who had been sitting behind the driver pulled out a pistol as he dropped, and he was now holding it, ready to fire. After the shot, it felt to Cesar as if time stood still for a second —for everything except the flashing lights in the distance. He took aim again, this time at the man behind the driver. He fired. And hit his target.

AUGUST 25, 12:52 AM

"There they are!" Miriam said. "Shoot at them!"

"How can I shoot at them from here?" Lettie asked. "All these trees and stuff. And the fence."

"Then we need to move." Noluthando.

"All together?" Miriam.

"Do you have a better idea?" Noluthando.

While this was going on, Lettie tried to hold the revolver in such a way that she could get a feel for how to shoot it across a greater distance. And to hit something. It felt strange to her. And somehow wrong. Wrong to consider how to kill other people. But wasn't that why they had come? To kill?

"If we can reach that spot," Lettie pointed at several bushes that were standing a fair distance from the fence. She made a sweeping gesture toward the path the women should take. "We could try from over there."

"Try what?" Princess.

"To shoot," Lettie said.

AUGUST 25, 12:51 AM

Vuyo was glad that he had smelled a rat. When the car with its lights off drove up, he turned around and crawled off in the other direction. He had a nose for danger.

Behind him, he heard a second shot go off one or two minutes after the last one, and on the horizon he saw something that gave him hope.

He crawled toward it.

AUGUST 25, 12:53 AM

The next shot sent Bulelani into a full nosedive. It wasn't the first one that had been fired tonight without him knowing where it came from. *But now,* he thought, *I'm losing control of everything.*

The dirt in the field that he was running across grew softer, but it had been a long time since he had given his shoes any thought. The instant the next shot was fired, he dove into the dirt. While he was still falling, it occurred to him that he was much closer to the farmhouse than he'd thought. And he caught sight of two people crouched in front of a white bakkie. One of them must have shot at him.

"Stop!" he cried, raising both hands. "It's me!"

He had no idea if this was a signal they would understand. In any case, they didn't fire again.

AUGUST 25, 12:54 AM

Pastor was surprised. He was already down one man, the one with the foul breath, and this despite the fact they had barely even gotten here. People called this No Man's Land, the space between two fronts. And he had a feeling that they weren't just at risk from two sides. The shot that took out his associate had definitely come from the house, but he also suspected there was danger from somewhere out here, too. He was well acquainted with his survival instinct, and he trusted it. Their enemies were sitting inside the house, but not everyone outside was necessarily on their side.

And behind them, the cops were on their way to the farm. He had given this some thought, and had come to the conclusion that he should have taken the two police vehicles more seriously.

Pastor was still kneeling behind the open driver's door. One of his associates had fired once.

"Stop!" he heard a voice. "It's me!"

AUGUST 25, 12:53 AM

Jayne felt her age as she stood up. The cold had seeped into her bones. She needed a few moments to even be able to stretch. A second shot was fired.

Whoever had been standing on the other side of the hedge had put some major distance between himself, her, and Thabo. As she considered running after him—after all, she believed he was the leader of the gang—she realized that something in this scene was off.

They had been involved in several firefights that had almost been like a war, but now only single shots were being fired. The first had been from Franz. She was convinced of that now. The second had come from someone else. A different sound, a different source. But if these shots were no longer being met with immediate, militaristic return fire, then that could only mean one thing. Nobody knew anymore who was friend or foe. They had to exploit this reality.

By the time the third shot was fired, Jayne was helping Thabo to his feet.

"We have to get out of here!" she said.

AUGUST 25, 12:54 AM

Jo-Jo was standing at the terrace door, staring out toward the gate. He knew that the people who had just arrived weren't on their side, so he could shoot at them.

He wasn't a brave man, that much he knew about himself. But if only for Lettie who was somewhere out there, he had to do his duty. Jo-Jo sprinted across to the bullet-ridden police car and crouched behind the trunk. Through the shattered windshield, he had a good view of the gate and the white bakkie that sat beyond it. No one was currently offering to sacrifice themselves to one of his bullets, but he would wait.

"Sssssst!" he heard from overhead. He looked up at the house and saw the Boss leaning out the window. Was he waving at him?

The Boss had never waved at him. Jo-Jo didn't wave back.

AUGUST 25, 12:54 AM

Cesar wasn't sure that he had shot the right man. The four who had driven up in the bakkie just now looked like people you ran into everywhere in the townships. Why should they shoot at them? *Well*, he thought, *the fact that they've shown up out here in the middle of the night is rather suspicious*. Why would they do that? He couldn't think of a reason.

With that, he raised his gun and fired one more time.

AUGUST 25, AFTER 12:54 AM

The shot that Cesar squeezed off missed its mark. The bullet grazed the roof of the bakkie with a loud *screeee* and vanished into the night without leaving a mark anywhere else.

This time Pastor immediately located where the shot had come from, and he returned fire. He pulled his semi-automatic gun out from under his seat and fired at the house. The guy with the terrible breath had been shot from that direction. *Something has to happen quickly either way*, Pastor thought. The cops were on their way.

Cesar dove sideways onto the floor and managed to shout, "Get down!" as a warning to Betsie, Trixie and the children. The majority of the bullets that Pastor fired buried themselves in the ceiling of the prayer room. One bullet bounced off a hinge on the window frame, missing Cesar by only a centimeter.

Sergeant Twaku could see the farmhouse as a silhouette against the horizon, and he dropped his speed once more. He was having difficulty distinguishing between light and dark colors, and he couldn't make out much more than a dark shadow in the distance. "Everything looks peaceful over there!" Van Vuuren's voice crackled through the radio. "Yeah," Constable Ncita said beside him. They would have heard the gunfire if they had been driving along with their windows down, as they usually did. But the night was chilly.

Hope triumphed over despair. The police were finally here. Vuyo had never been so happy to see their flashing lights. He had run from them many times before, but today was a different story. They could keep shooting behind him all they wanted.

Bulelani wasn't sure if his shout had reached anyone. He remained hidden behind a shrub, which was at least fifty meters away from the bakkie. The two shooters, one of whom had shot at him, were now cowering under the vehicle. He heard the bullet strike the roof and the shots as Pastor returned fire. And then the gunfire from wherever it was coming. It would be best for him to stay put.

Jo-Jo wasn't scared. Maybe that was because the Boss was watching out for him. He stretched out across the tail of the police BMW and aimed at the bakkie as well as he could. He could make out the white paint better than anything else. *If I hit the truck,* he thought, *then the odds are good that the tsotsis will also get some.* And so he fired. Thwap, thwap, thwap, thwap. Until he was out of bullets.

Crawling was painful for Vuyo. He struggled to get up on his feet and stretch. His back ached from the unaccustomed movement. And the leg with the bullet wound hurt. He put weight on both legs at the same time and groaned. Taking little strides, he reached the middle of the dusty road and spread out his arms. He could see the police car. *Oh,* he thought, *there are two of them.*

"Take your hands off my shoulders," Lettie said quietly. "What?" Princess asked loudly back in reply. Because of the noise of the shots, it had become harder to understand each other. Lettie pushed the other woman's hands off her shoulders and raised her arms so she had the revolver's trigger before her eyes. *Your eyes can adjust pretty well to the dark,* she thought. The two tsotsis they'd just seen had fallen back when the newcomers arrived, and now they were standing as far away from the fence as from the women. Lettie took her time to take aim and pull the trigger. One of the tsotsis instantly crumpled. The other jumped sideways. Lettie lowered the revolver, and then fired twice more even though she could no longer see the second gangster. "Try again!" she heard Noluthando behind her.

Franz Muller watched Jo-Jo used up the last of his ammunition. He was still at the same spot Jayne had assigned to him. She had somehow taken over the leadership position. Should he stay here? Or go somewhere else? He could try to lower his high-tech gun down to Jo-Jo on a rope. But wouldn't that be too dangerous for his worker? He would have to come over to get it. He could throw it down. Muller wondered who had just fired. He had identified three shots from an old, heavy revolver.

"Watch out!" Constable Ncita called.

But Sergeant Twaku had no eyes for the living

hindrance right in front of him. He hit Vuyo and drove right over him. Only then did he hit his brakes hard. "What was that?" he asked. "That was one of them," Ncita said. "That's what I said."

"Rescue!" was the next to last thing that Vuyo ever thought. And then, "Why aren't they stopping?" right before he was struck by the first police car. It drove over him, breaking multiple bones but not killing him. But then the second vehicle's front axle hit him in the head, and he died instantly. The old Nissan with Inspector van Vuuren at the wheel came to a stop across his body.

Pastor went on the defensive when they started shooting at his car. He didn't know if the other two men were still alive on the other side of the bakkie. There was shooting going on somewhere. Not far from him, but he couldn't zero in on exactly where. Or who was being shot at. Friend or foe? He had no idea. And now the police were also here. It would be enough for now if he could at least manage to keep their line of retreat open. He positioned himself behind the open rear door and aimed at the first police car.

"That's what I said!" As she said this, Constable Ncita opened her door and climbed out to examine the injured man. The bullet struck her underneath her double chin, knocking her to the ground. She died only seconds after the car hit Vuyo. Sergeant Twaku responded in the way he'd been trained at the police academy. He slid as far as possible from his seat onto the floorboard. As he did this, he turned off his headlights and flashers. Two bullets ricocheted sideways off the

windshield while two or three more flew off somewhere. He then opened the door, hoping that no
one from that side would shoot at him.

Thabo cursed the injury that he had received
all those years ago. Paralysis due to blood poi-
soning. Despite that, he was still quite mobile, but
Jayne was far ahead of him. He couldn't see her
anymore. What was going on at the house made
him nervous, but he couldn't move any faster. He
desperately wished he was in a safer location and
could make sure that the right ones got what was
coming to them. Bam, bam, one after the other.
He was out of breath and had to stop. He thought
he recognized the sound of the gun that had just
been fired three times. This didn't help him get his
anxiety back under control.

One thing was clear to Jayne. She wouldn't
find herself under fire from behind. Everything else
was a mystery to her. Jayne saw the flashing lights
without having a sightline on the cars. How did
the police get out here? The gunfire was coming
from all directions, going in all directions. She had
lost perspective. She assumed that her people
were the only ones shooting from inside the
fence line. But what did they see from there?
And besides the cops, were any other people
outside on her side? What had the worker said?
Was the woman he'd recognized actually his
wife? If so, then she had wandered off between
the two fronts. And the shadow up ahead. Was
that the ringleader? Why wasn't he over by the
people who had come in the bakkie? Jayne crept
slowly closer to the shadow.

It felt safer to crouch low to the ground. Less vulnerable. Bulelani watched the scene at the gate and wondered what had gone wrong. Why had Pastor come under fire the moment they got here? And was Pastor's accomplice who was lying across the passenger seat really dead? Where were Enoch and Sandi? And where was Lulama? How in the world had the cops made it out here? And what were the odds that he could get out of here? Bulelani was no longer thinking about the diamonds. Or about searching for money and jewelry inside the house. He had to get away. But where? If the cops stayed busy, maybe he could slip away down the side of the road. But he had no idea how many cops had come in the two cars. Now they were shooting at the bakkie. Better to find another way. Away from the road. Like he'd done earlier that evening when he'd run into the white farmer. He looked around. And was sure that he saw something move.

"Go!" Noluthando said from the back. *She has a point*, Lettie thought. She didn't have eyes in the back of her head, but she was certain that the three other women were lined up behind her. Behind her and the revolver. She had reloaded it and was slowly approaching the spot where she had just seen the two tsotsis. One of them had fallen over, and the other jumped to the side. Lettie was very scared.

Sergeant Twaku let himself tumble out of the car. As he landed on the ground, the glass in the driver's door was shot out. He looked over his shoulder. The driver's door on the second car was also open. He saw van Vuuren throw himself out of the vehicle. Twaku rolled across the ground and landed on his stomach, his gun raised. Training is training. He wished he understood what had just happened. And he wished he hadn't made those jokes about what was going on out here to his young colleague. He hadn't been able to check her pulse. Not in this shootout. But what had just bubbled out of her throat must have been blood. He suspected she had no chance of surviving. He slowly scooted on his back toward the back of the car. He glanced around once more. Van Vuuren was firing at the white bakkie. Constable Magwaca was kneeling behind the passenger door. He waved at her to join him. It was safer behind his Ford than behind her door. The right ammunition could slice through it. Twaku then stood up behind the Ford and braced his arms against the roof. He fired all he had at the bakkie before turning around. Magwaca was lying there with a gaping hole in her head.

Jayne saw the shadow stand up. This was the man they had to thank for all of this. She had the feeling he was looking right in her direction. He reached behind his back.

Lettie kept walking. Step after step. Her bullet had cost the tsotsi most of his skull. She had had no idea what the revolver could actually do. What bothered her even more though was the fact that the other man was nowhere to be seen. Nonetheless, there was still heavy gunfire in front of them, so they kept going. The other women followed her. The white bakkie was the vehicle that had just pulled up, and its arrival had changed everything. A thin man in a suit was kneeling at the driver's door and was firing toward the police cars. Lettie raised her arms and aimed. The helicopter returned. What were people who could afford something like that doing at this time of night? She took aim slowly and didn't pull the trigger until she was certain. The man in the suit crumpled into the car.

Bulelani was holding his pistol when he heard the chopper. *Absurd*, he thought. He had been so close and yet so far. He thought about the diamonds that were now on that helicopter, on their way to Mozambique. The crap doctor had mentioned the Mozambique mafia. *Next time*, Bulelani thought as he watched the helicopter fly over the farmhouse. He saw the lights slip away. What he didn't see was Jayne slipping up on him. She shot Bulelani twice in the heart.

The gunfire ended as the helicopter disappeared. Everything was completely quiet. But then Lettie heard Miriam start to weep behind her, even though there was no longer any reason to do that.

AUGUST 25, 2:49 AM

Enoch had stopped running a while ago. He was out of breath. It both ended and yet never ended, this farmland. *And everything still belongs to the whites,* he thought.

When it was all over, he didn't understand what had happened on the farm. When Sandi had been shot, he had jumped to the side. But he had still been splattered with his blood. It had sprayed that far. He had stayed on the ground for a minute, completely still, before deciding that the best thing was for him to just vanish. The power relations had changed. To their disadvantage. And even though the guys in the white bakkie might have been their backup, which they had never known for sure, the arrival of the cops had meant that everything was pretty much over.

What had happened to Bulelani?

Enoch laughed at the thought of how he had shot the female cop between the two cars. Bam. She had just toppled over. The cow.

Finally the county road. Somewhere along here was the second car, but Bulelani had the keys.

It was dark, and it could be a long time until a taxi came by. Besides, it might be a good idea not to board one anywhere around here. But it was a long way to Zwelitsha, and he didn't want to have to walk the whole distance.

When he got home, he would send the kids out of his shack and make love to his wife.

Thanks to Martin Baltes and Dorothee Plass, who accompanied this project and helped me to understand where I wanted to go with it.

And thanks to Henriette Gunkel, Anette Hoffmann, Dirk Lange, and Burkhard Schirdewahn, who read through my manuscript and improved it through their comments and critiques.

A huge thanks to Gary Minkley. For everything.